Sherwin A. Goodman

Rick Drago's

Hell In Paradise

Hell In Paradise

ISBN: 9781777536787

Chapter One

Antoine Bianco killed people for a living. He had a long list of illegal activities and was on the police watch list for a long time. They arrested him many times, and somehow he beats the rap each time with his high-priced lawyer.

The police had been after him for many years, but he always eluded being caught red-handed.

Rick Drago was about to save the police and the taxpayers' time and money in legal fees.

Dressed in a black combat suit with the tools of his trade, he padded towards the eastern side of the hilltop villa.

According to reliable information, Antoine Bianco had been living at that villa on the island of Trinidad for the past couple of weeks. Rick Drago hoped the intel was still good. There was no time to lose.

When the report came across Dan's desk, he knew who the man for the job would be.

Rick Drago had worked on the Caribbean islands before and still had contacts there. He readily accepted the mission, knowing he would see some old friends again.

The cool breeze greeted Rick Drago as he moved among the trees and small rocks. He was approaching the house from the east. No one was visible, and they turned the lights off inside the home. But that didn't mean a thing.

At the south corner of the grounds were a few tall coconut trees and mango trees.

Rick noticed it hung the branches low to the ground from the weight of the many mangos hanging from them.

Moving swiftly and low, Rick headed for the trees. He stopped and listened, a second landing at the western end of the house, but all he heard was the sound of cock crowing in the distance. Bianco had picked a prime place to hide out. The place was at the top of a hill and away from prying eyes. It was Maracas Bay, located in the North side of the island, close to a busy fishing village.

It will take about one hour's drive to reach the city of Port-of-Spain.

The view displayed only the villa on top of a

hill, but once up there, you can see it's a sprawling property with enough space to do gardening and other cultural work if you want to.

Many small fruit trees were growing on the grounds. Close to the southwest corner of the villa was a large gazebo with a swinging twin-seater chair covered with a canopy.

No one was visible. Rick Drago could see no movement inside the house. Drago was a little bothered, but not surprised that Antoine would be alone at the villa.

Rick Drago stayed put. As the time dragged by, he did not want to rush to the house until he was sure there was no security.

There was the ground floor and one other upper floor at the west end of the house. They had built the house like an L. Drago looked on.

Someone switched on a light and exposed a shadowy figure across the window at the other end of the house.

Drago couldn't tell if it was a man or a woman. From the silhouette, it appears the person carried a gun in a holster under the arm.

Could it be a guard? Or is it the man, Antoine Bianco?"

Drago thought to himself. Using the small fruit trees for cover, he crouched and moved closer to the dimly lit window.With his back to the wall, Drago tried to see through the tiny opening in the drawn window shade. As luck would have it for him, the door opened, and a person dressed in black clothing stepped out With his stiletto blade in hand, Drago's left hand took hold of the person's mouth as his right hand brought the stiletto blade across the throat.

Drago then dragged the body away from the door to the side of the building and out of sight. A quick search revealed that it was a man armed with a pistol and a radio tucked away under his jacket.

Drago thought to himself. If this guard is here on the east side of the house. There has to be one on the west side.

Rising, Drago moved as soundlessly as he could be with his back to the wall. He slipped along until he saw the last window on the west side.

Drago stopped and waited. Then he heard the radio as the guard tried to reach his counterpart.

Now. Drago knew where the guard was hiding away from anyone or anything approaching the villa from the west, which had the only road leading to and from the house.

Rick Drago was about to move when, out of the corner of his right eye, he glimpsed the movement of something.

A figure lunged at him, a blade glittering in

its hand. Rick pivoted as the knife passed near his face. Before the figure could swing again, Drago brought his stiletto into play, finding its mark in the person's jugular. The blade dropped from the person's hand as both hands tried to stop the gushing blood from their throat.

The body collapsed to the ground. There were much more shrubs on this side of the house, giving Drago more hiding space for this body.

Drago waited a few moments to verify that the area ahead was clear and safe. A door hung open a crack. Drago got on one knee and pushed the door, making it wide enough to get a better view of the inside.

Seeing and hearing no one, he entered. A burst of bullets missed his head, but not by much. He jumped to the right, using the stairs for cover as the gunman continued to fire.

Drago was combat-ready with his special 9mm and silencer attached. He fired three quick rounds at the shooter. A scream, then a crashing sound as the man fell and tumbled down the stairs, landing inches away from Drago.

Drago searched the body and found a driver's license in the name of Ryan Gallagher.

Irish. What is an Irish gunman doing here with Bianco? Drago thought to himself. Could it be that Antoine Bianco is working for the Irish family?

Drago paused on the bottom step. Then climbed slowly, and he kept looking up. The stairwell curved to the left, ending at a landing where the Uzi, with a silencer attached, fell from the Irishman's hand after being shot by Drago.

Reaching the last step, Drago peaked over the landing. An empty floor leading to the left greeted him. Only a door at the end of the hall with an exit sign above was visible. Drago picked up the Uzi. He checked the magazine. Plenty of firepower was still in it. Drago holstered the 9mm and swung the Uzi over his shoulder.

Staying low, Drago moved along the hallway, heading for the door. The sound of a powerful engine and tires eating gravel came from outside. Drago thrusts open the door and release a burst of lead from the Uzi at the speeding car. Bullets hit the car, damaging the rear lights.

Drago sprinted after the speeding car and continued firing from the Uzi until he heard the clanging sound of the empty chamber. Rick Drago came to an abrupt stop, inhaling deeply, and tossed the Uzi in the bushes at the side of the road. "Damn!" he said.

Drago wasn't sure if he had hit the person driving the vehicle.

That had to be Bianco driving the get-away car. Drago speculated. Why did Bianco not return fire when Drago shot at him and ran away? Something big was about to happen, and Bianco was sure he was fit and available.

Drago searches the rooms, starting with the only room on the floor that Bianco occupied. He hoped to find a clue why the hit-man didn't get into an altercation with him.

Drago found bits of paper in the garbage can, confirming that Bianco was working for the Irish family.

Satisfied with the information his search provided. Drago left the villa.Today is one of those days that Dan McCall wishes he was still working out in the field. Instead, he is heading for the office. His cell phone hasn't stopped buzzing since the early morning hours.

Dan had worked late at the office the previous day, catching up with long overdue paperwork. He had only returned from his trip to Asia one day before.

They backed the traffic up on Route 125, caused by road repairs. Sitting in his car, the call he'd been waiting for came. It was Drago calling.

"Yes, Dan here," McCall said.

"How are you?" Drago asked, knowing Dan had just returned from his trip to Asia.

"Tired. Wishing I was with you at this moment, enjoying the Caribbean atmosphere.

"The weather here is beautiful. That's the only good thing."

"Sounds like you are on the move."

"Yes. I am."

"Where to?"

"A search. Running wild," Drago said.

"Running wild?" (Code for target has eluded him and was on the move)

"Yes."

"How long ago?"

"30 Minutes to an hour."

"The enforcer could be anywhere at this moment."

"I have an idea where he is going. Although he may decide not to go there," Drago said.

"I am minutes away from the office. Check with me later."

McCall entered and sat behind the desk in his office. The papers he had left the night before were still on his desk. He buzzed his secretary, Dorothy Adams.

**Chapter Two**

Dorothy Adams, a long military career woman, was one of the toughest drill sergeants in the military. She has done two active tours of duty before becoming a drill sergeant. She has never been married and has one daughter fifteen years of age.

Dorothy Adams has been with Dan McCall for the past three years. She entered McCall's office carrying a notepad and pen, with glasses stuck on her forehead.

"Yes, Dan," Dorothy said as she entered the office.

McCall had instructed the people working with him to use his first name.

"Where is Drago now?"

"Last report, he was heading towards Tobago."

"What about the enforcer? Any word on him?"

"No. Nothing as yet."

"Give that a priority. I don't need Rick to be in the blind and running wild," Dan instructed.

"Will do," Dorothy replied, then turned and left the office.

Officer Gene Livingston knocked on McCall's office door.

"Come in!" Dan reply.

Gene enters carrying a sheet of paper with a printout on it.

"Yes. What is it?" Dan asked.

"This just came in. I thought you should look at it."

McCall took the printout and looked at it. A private jet crashed on approach to the airstrip at Jamaica Airport. They presume all the passengers on board are dead.

The private jet crashing was news, but what

made it more interesting were the names of the passengers on board.

Among the people on board were Dobbie Flanagan, James O'Neill, and four unidentified women.

Dobbie and James were two well-known men to the many law enforcement agencies as members of Irish families.

Coincidence is something that McCall does not believe in. An enforcer for the Irish is on the Island of Trinidad accompanied by bodyguards seems odd. Or was it a hit team working for the Irish family to carry out a job too big for one man.

And now a private jet crashed on approach to the landing strip in Jamaica with high-ranking members from the Irish community on board.

Something big was going to happen on one of the Caribbean Islands.

McCall left his office. He took the elevator to the basement floor and entered the comm room. A stocky man greeted him.

"How are things? Dave?" McCall asked.

McCall has known Dave Griffin from the first day he entered the office fresh out of the academy. Dave was among the top five graduates in communication skills. He is a fourteen-year veteran of the justice department.

McCall has called upon him on many

occasions. Now he wanted the exact location of his man, Rick Drago.

Dave Griffin sat down at his desk. McCall sat across from him and watched Dave punch in numbers and figures.

"He is on the Sir Solomon Highway heading to Tobago."

"Can you find the enforcer he is trying to find?"

"Name."

"Antoine Bianco," McCall said.

"Nothing new," Dave replied. "Last confirmation was here, at the Villa in the Maracas Bay area."

Dave pointed at the screen and enlarged the photo of the house.

"The enforcer has dumped everything," McCall implied.

"That's the usual, isn't it?" Dave questioned.

"Yes."

McCall got up and left Dave's office. He called Drago.

"Hello," Drago answered.

"We have nothing on your man," McCall said.

*Trinidad & Tobago*

"I'm heading to Tobago."

"Why?"

"Pieces of paper I found in the wastebasket have Tobago written on it, and another has Couva," Drago stated.

"What's in Couva?"

"I think it's a sea-port."

"You think he was planning on leaving the island by sea?"

"Not sure."

"A private jet crashed in Jamaica, and two passengers were members of the Irish family, Dobbie Flanagan, and James O'Neill."

"Jamaica?"

"Any other heads of families coming to the Islands?"

"We are working on it. I will get back to you when we have confirmation."

"Got it," Drago said.

An enforcer in the Caribbean and a plane crash in Jamaica with members of a crime family on board, coincidence? McCall never believed in coincidences.

The quaint resort was famous for the length and purity of its beaches. Montego Bay was now busier than ever, bustling with tourists for the casinos.

Danny O'Brien stood on the balcony of his room in the Grand Hotel and gazed out over the beach and Caribbean ocean. Jamaica! he thought to himself. What a beautiful place to live.

He had been in the country only a while and was fond of the island.

The island possessed something that fascinated O'Brien. He could feel it in his body as the sun and wind beat on his face and naked upper body.

A much healthier climate here than in the stuffy and muggy city of Malahide, the place he calls home.

Danny O'Brien was here to meet with a man he had never seen. He is here for the Irish organization in the United States of America. He wondered why he couldn't meet with the person in America, but he knew not to question his uncle's decisions about matters that concerned the family.

On his first night on the island, O'Brien had strolled through the shanty town districts and mingled with the hookers and tough guys. He wanted the feel for the excitement of the culture he knew about.

It was a plus for Danny, the feeling that came over him on his first visit to Jamaica. He had never expected to find such an atmosphere so much like the one he grew up knowing.

Back in the city of Malahide, things were a little different, but in the end, the outcome was similar.

Here on the island, people are never in a hurry. They went about their duty in a carefree mood. Their elders handed it down through the generations for years.

The Caribbean island and their counterparts in South America are very much alike. The only difference was the siesta time in South America.

The Caribbean islands were unique. Danny could see himself living and enjoying life here. The sound of the ringing telephone in his suite broke his musing.

He strode into his room and answered the phone call.

"Hello," Danny said after picking up the receiver.

"You have visitors," the receptionist said.

"Okay, send them up!"

The visitors weren't the people Danny expected when he opened the door of his room.

"Who are you? And what can I do for you?" Danny asked, looking at the tall man in the company of four heavy-set men.

Noel Charles grew up on the streets of Spanish Town, one of the deadliest districts in Jamaica. Noel was in the drug business from age thirteen when he began selling his school friends ten cents spiffs.

Now. Charles has a crew and has made a name for himself in the drug trade business in the Caribbean. Charles also has one of the deadliest posse throughout the region.

"Who am I?"

"What can I do for you?"

"It's not what you can do for me. I am here to do something for you."

"What can you do for me?"

"I can give you good advice."

"Is that a habit of yours? Giving a stranger good advice?"

"Only those trying to do business on my turf without permission."

"I am here on a vacation. I do not know where you got the impression that I was here on business."

"Keep it that way!" One of Charles men stated.

"Let's take a ride!" Charles suggested.

The six men left the room and took the service elevator to the ground floor, where the two dark-colored SUVs with tinted windows parked.

Noel Charles, Danny O'Brien, and two bodyguards got into one vehicle. The other two bodyguards got into the other SUV and drove off.

Antoine Bianco boarded a Liat plane at the ANR Robinson International Airport in Crown Point in Tobago for his flight to Jamaica.

A gathering of family heads from Arizona had descended on the Cayman Islands. That was the printout that Dorothy brought into Dan McCall's office late on Tuesday afternoon.

"Contact Drago!" McCall ordered.

Moments later, the phone in McCall's office buzzed.

"Hello," Dan said when he picked up the receiver and answered the phone.

"Drago is on line two," Dorothy explained.

"Cayman Islands," McCall said.

"What's on the Cayman Islands?" Drago asked.

"I believe that's where the action will take place. Many heads of families are gathering there."

"Cayman Islands. Jamaica is close to the Cayman," Drago said.

"Yes."

"Understand. On my way," Rick Drago said.

"Petrov not here yet?" Fedorov asked, annoyed.

Igor Volkov. A junior member of the Russian organization whose appetite for viciousness matched Fedorov's answer.

"He should be here soon, boss. The plane will pick him up on schedule."

Fedorov sighed and walked out to the balcony.

The rented villa prided itself on providing every luxury to its guest. It was large even to accommodate eight people.

A swimming pool and sauna. A staff of four people, two maids to keep the rooms tidy and clean, and two people in the kitchen.

Fedorov re-entered the room and looked at his comrades.

"As you all suspected," he said gravely. "It has begun, even as I speak to you. Three heads of the Irish family have been taken care of on the coast of Jamaica."

"And that's just the beginning," Igor Volkov assured the others.

"Before the end of this week, we hope to be rid of many heads of the Irish organization."

"Soon, they will be leaderless," Fedorov proudly said.

The other members of the group nodded and smiled with admiration. As always, they hung on every word Fedorov said.

"Petrov has arrived," a young lieutenant said as he opened the door where Fedorov and the others gathered.

Petrov entered the house, followed closely by two of his most trusted lieutenants.

One of Petrov's men, Andrei Popov, stood six feet five inches with a muscular frame and weighed two hundred and thirty pounds.

Popov grew up on the streets of Magadan and was second in command to one of the most dangerous gangs in the area.

The other lieutenant. Ivan Ivanov's nick-named Eye-eye. Like Andrei, Ivan grew up on the streets and was a member of various street gangs before finding a home with the Russian mob.

Like Fedorov, Petrov had surrounded himself with young men like himself, men with violent natures unmatched by many.

"Have you heard anything new, Petrov?" Fedorov asked.

"Yes. The news is, the Irish are bringing in new members from Dublin," Petrov said.

"They will outnumber us. We will have to do the same or use our brains instead of brawls and outwit them," Fedorov suggested.

"Not only are they bringing in more muscle from across the pond, but they are also teaming up with one of Jamaica's most feared possies," Petrov stated.

"What day do our other members scheduled to arrive?" Fedorov asked.

"The New Mexico group will be here tomorrow. The Californians are due the following day," Igor Volkov replied.

"The longer we wait for our members to arrive, it becomes more dangerous. The Irish could strike back at any moment while we sit here waiting," Fedorov stated.

**Chapter Three**

'I am not worried," Igor boasted. "You've never let us down yet, and I am sure you never will."

"That's with my family, but this involves the decision of all the other families."

"Some of what you are saying is true, Fedorov. But, like us, the Irish are also waiting for the recruits from across the pond," Petrov said.

"What about the Jamaicans? How come we didn't think about having them on our side? They could have been a great help to us," Fedorov said.

The mood in the room among the members present was upbeat. Fedorov was pleased. Looking around, he could see it on their faces. A sensation of achievement washed over him, tingling his entire body.

At that moment, the house phone rang. Igor Volkov answered. "Okay. Thank you," he said and hung up the receiver.

"Who was on the phone?" Fedorov asked.

"That was the delivery people. The items you ordered will be here within the hour."

"You were about to say something, Petrov," Fedorov said.

"It's too late for that now. The Irish got to them first," Petrov stated.

### Cayman Islands

Rick Drago arrived in the Cayman Islands. He checked into The Grand Cayman Beach and Resort Spa.

At the receptionist's desk, a care package was waiting for him, which contained the tools of his trade.

In his suite, Drago took a shower. Then he opened a mini bottle of whiskey. Also in the package, Drago found the mug-shots of six men with their names written at the back of the photos.

Drago gulped the last of his Jack Daniels whiskey, savoring the taste as it went down his throat. He studied the photos and the names, then destroyed them.

James Murphy took the elevator from the penthouse of Hotel Grand Casino and Spa to the first floor. Flanked by two burly black bodyguards, he entered a room that displayed the Restricted sign. Hotel employees only.

The two bodyguards. Arley Campbell stood six foot five inches and weighed two hundred and forty pounds.

Tarone Davis stood six foot one inch and

weighed two hundred and fifty pounds. The two young men were inseparable from their days at school.

The guards stood outside the door after searching and making the room safe for Murphy to enter.

Murphy has his private entrance from that room to the Casino and the sorting room where the cash is counted and stacked.

James Murphy made that trip every day at the same time. He liked to watch the receipts of the day counted by the staff. Some staff members believed he was always there to see how much he would skim before signing off the day's receipts.

James Murphy has two loves. Money and women in that order, and he didn't care about how it got anyone of them. Loansharking, money laundering using the hotel to launder illegal funds, Murphy would do it for a piece of the action.

Nicholas Clarke was on hand, overseeing the counting of the daily casino receipts.

"Good day, sir," Nicholas said.

Murphy smiled and shook Nicholas's hand. "How was today?"

"We had a good day."

"Great. That's what I like to hear."

Clarke had heard those words from Murphy

many times. He smiled, walked with his boss to the cubicle where Murphy sits, and watched the staff as they counted the daily receipts.

The cubicle walled in by bulletproof glass. It was a small room decorated with one table, two chairs, and a tiny refrigerator.

Murphy sank into the cushions on his lazy-boy chair and enjoyed the sight of cash on the table counted.

"Bring me a cup of coffee," he said.

Clarke left the room.

Murphy's cell phone rang. "Yes," he answered.

"Where are you?"

"Where I always am at this time every day, Marcia."

Marcia Campbell, a thirty-something brown skin buxom Jamaican woman, was on the other end of the phone call.

Marcia caught the eye of Murphy on her first night performing at the Casino. At the end of her singing performance, Murphy sends a message for her to join him in his private office. It was love at first sight.

"What time is your flight?" Murphy asked.

"Six am."

"Okay. Have a safe flight. I will see you when you get back."

"I will stay a few days after the funeral."

"Yes. I remember. Take as much time as you need with your family."

"I wanted to hear your voice before I leave."

"I understand. Take care," Murphy said, then turn off his cell phone.

Nicholas Clarke returned with a pot of coffee, two cups, and a bottle of Irish whiskey.

"Let's relax and enjoy this moment!" Murphy suggested, pouring coffee into one cup and a splash of whiskey.

Nicholas did the same. The two men sat back and looked at the money on the table.

"Anything new from Noel Charles?" Murphy asked.

"Tomorrow. he will let me know about the progress made."

"No mistakes."

"Noel is not a man who makes mistakes. He is a reliable person."

"Good. It is payback time."

"When will the others arrive?" Clarke asked.

"Day after tomorrow," Murphy replied.

Others expecting were heads of the New Mexico Irish families. Among them was Rian Murphy, the older brother of James Murphy. When the family invested money in the hotel in Jamaica, it was Rian who made it possible for James to oversee the day-to-day running of the Grand Casino and Spa.

Antoine Bianco checked into the Grand Casino and Spa. He entered the suite reserved for him and dropped his one piece of luggage on the carpeted floor.

The suite had a large flat-screen TV. A king-size mattress, a bed, and a mini-bar.

The enforcer dialed the cell number after checking into his suite.

James Murphy answered his phone. "Yes."

"Murphy, this is Bianco."

The tone of the enforcer's voice was more eloquent than Murphy had ever heard.

"What's wrong?" Murphy asked.

"The other guys didn't make it."

"That is not good. We have lost many excellent soldiers and heads of family members," James said.

"Yes. I am aware of it."

"Who did it?" James Murphy asked.

"I am not sure. I think it was an American."

"American? You sure about that?"

"Who else could it be? The Russians would never send one man on a job like that."

"American! That means we have a bigger problem on our hands. Like the Russians, no family would send one man. That means it is the government, a specialist," James Murphy suggested.

"I have heard about an agent that operates

here in the Caribbean, but I have never seen him or have any information," Bianco said.

"Okay. I will make a few calls and get back to you."

The line went dead. Deeply frustrated, James Murphy got up from his seat.

"I am going out for some fresh air, Clarke. Have the final tally brought to my suite. I will join you later," Murphy said.

Murphy had a strange feeling of relentlessness. The news from Bianco about an American at the house in Trinidad was not good.

Was the American D.E.A. or a C.I.A. operative? Either way. If the Americans were involved, the problem now got difficult.

"What's wrong? Boss?" one bodyguard asked when Murphy stepped out of the room.

"Just need a little fresh air, nothing to worry about," Murphy replied.

The guards knew better. They know Murphy never leaves the counting room until everything is complete. And he doesn't go outside for fresh air. Murphy takes that from the balcony of his suite.

Arley Campbell and Tarone Davis glued to Murphy like fleas on a hound dog. They went out of the private entrance and entered the parking garage. Tarone slid behind the wheel of the Mercedes Benz. Arley opened the back door for the boss and then sat in the front passenger seat.

"Where to, Boss?" he asked.

Murphy had no particular place to go. His woman Marcia was due to leave the island on a six am flight.

"Drive. I'll let you know when to stop. I need to clear my head."

Tarone did as instructed. He knew his boss loved the scenery on Negril Road. It has been a long time since he took the view of the district.

Murphy rolled down the car window and felt the fresh, salty air on his face.

Changes made along the route. Units of bungalows replaced the shacks and shanty houses. Now displaying for rent signs.

James Murphy reached into his jacket for a Panetela cigar. He loves the taste of the long, thin cigars from South America. James pushes into the car cigar lighter. The lighter created a spark and a puff of smoke. It happened so fast that Murphy had no time to react or say anything to his bodyguards.

The explosion ripped the back half of the Mercedes Benz with minimal damage to the front of the vehicle. The blast sent the two bodyguards hurling through the air, landing ten feet from where the other half of the car was in flames.

James Murphy's body was chew into tiny pieces along with the back end of the car.

## *NEW YORK*

At 3;00 AM, the phone rang. Dan McCall reached over to the nightstand and picked up the receiver. "Hello."

"Good morning, sir. You asked to be notified if anything came in from the Caribbean Islands."

McCall left the bed and walked over to his desk, carrying the phone receiver. It was the night duty agent on the other end of the line. Tim Hargrove, a six-year veteran with the elite branch of the agency, was hand-picked by McCall for his present job.

"What is it? Do you have something?" McCall asked. His brain was now fully awake.

"Reports out of Jamaica. Turn on your television! sir!"

"What channel?"

"CNN, sir."

"Any word from Drago?" McCall asked.

"No."

McCall shuffled into his living room and turned on the television.

A reporter stood with a microphone in his hand. Behind him was what looked like a car in flames. Emergency crews ran around in the background as the cameraman zoomed in on the vehicle. McCall listened to the reporter. Only then did he realize why the agent had woken him.

The reporter was describing the event happening in the background.

James Murphy. The boss of Jamaica's largest gambling casino was killed in the explosion. His two bodyguards were thrown free, sustaining minor injuries.

## Chapter Four

McCall got back on the phone. "Hello, are you there, Tim?"

"Yes, sir." Hargrove paused. "I'm here."

"Contact Drago! He should be in the Cayman Islands. I want to speak to him."

"Will do."

Rick Drago glanced at the time display on his cell phone and answered it. "Hello."

"Drago. McCall wants to talk to you. Hold on while I patch you through."

"Have you heard about the car bombing in Jamaica?" McCall asked.

"Tidbits here and there," Drago said. "It appears, that the Russians have stepped up their plan of attack on the Irish."

"Any word on the date and time the bosses

will gather for the big meeting?" McCall asked.

"The buzz here is. Some bosses are worried about the meeting and if they will have enough soldiers for security protection."

"Did you get a look at the compound where the meeting will take place?"

"It's a kind of oceanfront compound with two huge villas."

"If an attack is going to be on the compound, it would come from the sea."

"Yeah. That's the logical entry. But the Irish could surprise everyone by attacking from the least expected point, by vehicle convoy," Drago suggested.

"What about the Irish enforcer? Anything on his whereabouts?" McCall asked.

"I think he is still in Jamaica. He will have to take charge of the team now that James Murphy has gone to meet his maker or until one of the big bosses arrives there."

"The Russians seemed to have a well-oiled machine hitting their targets with precision, and what I saw on the news about the car bombing in Jamaica, they also have a bomb expert at their disposal."

"Yes."

"The Italians are staying away from this one."

"They are probably waiting to see who will

come out ahead between these two families and then make their move on the winner."

"It will be a wait-and-see situation," Drago stated.

"Remember Rick. Your priority target is the enforcer, Antoine Bianco," McCall reminded him.

"But of course. I remember."

'We don't know what to expect from the Russians going up against the Irish. With the Italians, we always knew the body count would be high each time there's a mob war between two families."

There were times, like now, when the status quo bothered McCall even more than usual, not knowing if this fighting between the Russians and the Irish would bring a senseless loss of innocent lives.

There is nothing good about turf war. The only good about this, it wasn't taking place on American soil.

Results are the same wherever it is happening. Paradise Islands in the Caribbean, people go there to get away from the hustle and bustle of their hectic working hours, now have to be aware of where to go hoping not to be caught in the crossfire of the Russian/Irish vendetta.

Rick Drago pondered for a few seconds, then contented himself, knowing he only had to concentrate on Antoine Bianco. But, should anyone gets in the way of him carrying out his assignment, he would eliminate them. He hoped it wouldn't take long before the enforcer would show up on the Cayman Islands.

"You've never gone up against them before," McCall said.

"No. Not in a gang war."

"Odds are you might not have to this time around, either."

"Only if they get in my way of taking out Antoine Bianco," Drago said.

The Cayman Islands, like other Caribbean islands, was another tourist mecca with many places of entertainment.

The Caymans are situated 234 miles northeast of Jamaica. Whether you are looking for complete relaxation, exquisite dining, vibrating nightlife, or the underwater sights of the reefs, the cosmopolitan atmosphere of Grand Cayman has something for everyone.

Drago wore a multi-color short-sleeve shirt and white pants, a straw hat with matching sandals, a pair of binoculars, and a camera around his neck.

Drago's outfit gave the appearance of the typical tourist on vacation, enjoying the atmosphere and everything the island offers. He had a change of clothing in the trunk of the rental car he'd driven from the airport. The car was parked about a hundred feet away at the public entrance to the beach.

Drago parked the vehicle and walked along the beach. Other people were doing the same, walking and taking photos of the area and people enjoying the water sports.

There had been a break in the car bombing in Jamaica that took the life of James Murphy. A minor one, but a break is a break, doesn't matter how large or small.

The Jamaican C.I.D sector had received a call from a local cab driver. The cabby claimed to have seen the person that planted the car bomb, but he wasn't sure if it was a man or a woman. He stated that the person was of regular height and build, wearing dark clothing and a hoodie.

When the desk sergeant read the report, he immediately contacted his cousin Andrew Nolan, a member of Interpol, working in the Caribbean. He'd heard the rumor around the office that organized crime was responsible for the car bombing, and now a witness has come forward with information about seeing the person that put the bomb in the car.

That information to the Interpol agent in the Caribbean also came across the desk of the duty agent at the A.W.B headquarters office in New

York.

The A.W.B sector had done some digging and discovered that James Murphy had cheated many prominent business people out of millions of dollars before he became the boss of the casino in Jamaica.

So here McCall was, late in the evening, with a stack of papers on his desk. Among them was a transcript copy of the report sent to Interpol. The other was about James Murphy and his involvement many years ago with a housing scheme in Arizona where people lost millions of dollars.

McCall was going through the list of names in the file, some of which now hold important positions in the present government.

McCall had earlier sent the information to Drago.

Rick Drago was back in his suite at The Grand Cayman Beach and Resort Spa. The Fixer had just returned to his suite after viewing the villa the Russians had rented from the beachside. Drago had earlier driven along the beachfront and looked at the area. At the time, one vehicle was parked at the villa, and no guards were visible, not to say they weren't anyone posted.

Drago would do the Irish a favor and eliminate one of the Russian bosses for them, even the score.

Leaving his suite, Drago went along the beach. Here he was, eleven o'clock at night, moving swiftly between the sandbanks.

The 9mm with a silencer attached, nestled in a holster under his left arm, the .45 caliber strapped to his right hip.

Reaching the last sandbank at the back entrance to the villa, Drago stopped and listened. No sound came from inside. Drawing the .45 A.C.P Caliber pistol with the silencer attached. Drago reached the gate at the entrance leading from the two villas to the beach. He giggled the latch until the gate opened. Drago went around the small patio of the first villa that faced the ocean.

The cottage was in darkness. A sliding door at the back gave no resistance when Drago tugged on it. Putting on his night vision glasses, he searched the four bedrooms.

Drago took photos of the papers he found in the rooms. He then moved to the second villa. One of the rooms dimly lit.

He entered the kitchen, and a half-eaten sandwich lay on a plate. Drago touched the pot of coffee was still hot. In the living room he found two crates on the floor with papers scattered on the lids.

Drago left the living room looking for the person who had left the half-eaten sandwich in the kitchen. In the first bedroom, Drago found a man lying on his side. He turned the man onto his back.

"Who are? The man didn't get to finish the query.

"I'll ask the questions," Drago informed the man with the nozzle of the .45 up against his temple.

"What do you want?"

"Who are you? And where are the others?" Drago asked.

Before the man could answer, the growl of car engines heralded the arrival of vehicles.

Drago squeezed a bullet into the temple of the man. He rushed to the window as gravel crunched under the vehicle tires. Slipping out, he closed the window, hearing brakes. Then voices murmured.

Drago sprinted to the corner of the cottage. Not knowing who the arrivals at the villa were, he assumed they would enter through the front door. But he was wrong. Their murmured talk grew louder as they got closer to the corner of the villa.

The group was coming around the patio.

Drago squatted, three people appeared. They outfitted all the people in dark clothing. Two of them carried machine guns, while another had a large handgun.

Drago thought the gun could be a .45 magnum.

The Fixer was as still as a concrete pillar. The man carrying the handgun picked the lock of the sliding door and entered. Two others trailed him into the cottage.

Drago couldn't get past without being seen. His only option was to go back under the window and around the sandbank and tangled broad-leaf vines.

The fixer started to do so when the flash of gunfire reflected through the window.

Then one man spoke. "Getting even has a great feeling."

"Yes. Karma is a bitch," the other said in an Irish drawl.

The crew had just shot a man lying in bed, not knowing the man was already dead.

Usually, a hit team has a capo, a leader who knows what to look for and guides the others to carry out the mission successfully.

"Brian, did you see that?" Connor asked.

"See what? I didn't see anything, Connor," Brian replied.

"I saw something, or someone moved behind the sandbank."

"Let's check it out," Connor suggested.

"No. We should leave. We did the job. Let's get out of here!" the other man stated.

"What if it's a person, and they saw what we did?" Brian asked.

"He is right. We have to make sure. No witnesses, remember!" Connor remarked.

"Okay," the other man agreed. "Let's check it out."

Drago stayed crouched behind the sandbank.

"Come out," Brian shouted. "We have you surrounded."

The fixer raised his head high enough to see where the men were. One of them was about twelve feet away, and with the silencer attached to his weapon, he fired one bullet, hitting the man in the leg.

"I took a bullet in my leg," Connor yelled out. "He shot me."

"What direction did the shot come from?" Brian asked.

"I am not sure. It happened so fast. I can't tell," Connor said.

"This is the reason I said we should leave."

## Chapter Five

Drago crawled away from his position behind the sandbank and the long vines.

"Who are you?" Brian asked loudly.

"I am not here for you," Drago replied. He continued crawling away.

"I am losing a lot of blood. Let's go!"

Connor said.

Brian and the other man helped Connor to their vehicle. Brian slid in behind the wheel. He peeled out of the driveway and headed west.

The ocean tide had come further on the shore and brought along seaweeds. In the seaweeds were black urchins, what the locals call (black sea eggs). These urchins, if stepped upon, can cause considerable pain. The residents say to get the urchins out of your foot. You must walk on the hot tar road and let the heat bring the black needles from your foot.

Drago used the bright moonlight and avoided the seaweeds that washed ashore on the beach. The high tide had washed away the footprints in the sand.

He hurried to the sedan parked in the public parking area about twenty feet from the beach villa, where he encountered the Irish hit team and waited. He had enough time to change the wet clothes for drier pants and a shirt.

The headlights of a vehicle came on. It was a distance down the road. Drago believed it was the vehicle carrying the Irish team.

He didn't start the engine until the Irish vehicle passed his position, and the taillights were the size of a penlight.

Gunning it, he slewed up onto the freeway and rapidly accelerated. There was no need to drive any faster. The Irish were traveling at the posted speed limit, apparently to avoid attracting the attention of the local traffic police. He could hang back and keep them in his view.

Drago had closed the distance to keep them in sight. He always permitted at least two vehicles to come between them.

The situation changed once they reached the city. The traffic was heavy through the center of Bodden Town.

It did not surprise Drago when the Irish men passed through the town and continued west. He was expecting them to stop in Banksville to get medical attention for Connor, but they never did.

He concluded they were going directly to where they were staying without stopping.

Although the traffic had thinned outside the town, the driver hugged the slow lane and stayed within the posted speed limit.

Drago had hung back when he saw their braking, and the left signal light began to flash. He killed the engine and coasted to a stop under the branches of a tree overhanging the street.

The Irishman never noticed him. He locked the doors, took a camera, acting like a visiting tourist, and glided along the side of the road until he was at the entrance where the vehicle had turned.

Drago was about to enter when he noticed an

approaching car with the lights flashing, indicating to enter through the gate.

They made the fence around the building of wire and bushy small trees. Drago casually walked on, acting as if he wasn't interested in the cottage.

After the car had entered through the gate, Drago found a hole near the bottom of the fence. Seemingly barely big enough for a small kid to go through.

Scouring the street for pedestrians and seeing there were none. Drago dropped to his knees and pried at the open hole to widen it.

The building was vast and had two storeys.

There were many vehicles parked in the yard. Several were cars, one pickup, and one utility van. Drago took many pictures with the camera using the infrared lens. Four people got out of the newly arrived car. Drago continued using the camera. He took as much footage as he could, trying to focus on the faces of the occupants and the license plate from the vehicle that had just arrived.

The fixer returned to his hotel suite, poured himself a shot of Jack Daniels, and drank it in one gulp.

He then poured another and checked the footage he had taken of the cottage.

So, you have arrived," Drago said to himself

after seeing the face of Antoine Bianco (AKA The Enforcer)on the footage.

The enforcer was Noel Charles, Jamaica's number one gangster. His drug empire was crumbling. The Russians began intercepting his products before they reached the paying customers.

Noel Charles went to his good friend James Murphy and made a deal to have the Irish help him get his products into the Arizona market. And that's what started the conflict between the two families.

Danny O'Brien was also a member of the newly arrived group. The Irish had now even the odds for the loss of James Murphy, who was one of their leaders before a car bomb took his life in Jamaica.

Drago sent the footage to Dan McCall. Then he took a shower, drank the other Jack Daniels, and went to bed for a much-needed rest after the hectic day.

The fixer was up early the next day. He dressed in a bathing trunk, with a beach towel on his shoulder, and took a stroll on the beach. Many hotel guests were also out early on the beach. Some were jogging, and others were swimming in the sea as the tide returned to normal.

Hotel employees were clearing the area of

the seaweeds that came ashore with the high tide. The workers carefully handle the black sea eggs, placing them in pan carts and hauling them from the beach.

The fixer found a vacant beach chair and table. Drago sat down and gazed out over the sea, which was now calm.

A tall blonde woman rose from the other beach chair and walked towards Drago. She had a neat, commendable figure that seemed well-proportioned. In her late twenties, she had medium-length hair and blue eyes that were forthright.

The top and bottom she wore looked well on her. She had a gracious smile as she offered her hand.

"Rick?"

"Yeah. How do you do?" Drago asked.

"You don't remember me, do you?"

"Uh, give me a moment!"

"Valerie Morris. We met in Barbados at a party I was at with my friend Kayla."

"Oh, yes, of course. It is a pleasure seeing you."

"The pleasure is all mine. What are you doing here?"

"I am here on business," Drago replied.

"You know, that night in Barbados, I had my eye on you first, but you had eyes only for

49

Kayla."

"Well," he said, flushing slightly. You are correct, I didn't realize that you were interested in me from the way you were holding my friend Michael Strong."

"Michael. Yes, he's one hell of a man."

"What about you? Why are you here?" Drago asked.

"I am working. Leaving tomorrow after the shoot."

"Uh."

"Too bad we didn't meet a few days ago," Valerie stated.

"Have a safe travel," Drago said. "I will let Kayla know that I saw you here."

"No. Don't do that. Kayla might think that I took this assignment knowing you were here. I told her after the first night that I wanted to get to know you better. She replied, HANDS OFF."

"Goodbye, Valerie."

Drago returns to his suite after the early morning stroll on the beach. He ordered room service breakfast.

Wait for the meal to arrive. Drago put through a call to his father in Arizona, Thomas Drago.

"Hello, Rick," his dad said.

"Hi, Dad. How are you?"

"I am good. Where are you?"

"In the Cayman Islands at the moment," Rick replied.

"When will you be back?"

"Not sure."

"Take care."

"Always do," Rick said before turning off the phone.

A wrap on the door got his attention as he was about to make another call.

Drago walked to the door. "Yes," he answered.

"Your breakfast is here," the waiter said.

After breakfast, two slices of grain toast with marmalade, two poached eggs, a glass of orange juice, and a cup of coffee.

Drago calls his fiance Kayla Grandison in London.

"Hi, Hun," Kayla said.

"Just checking in with you."

"When are you coming home?" Kayla asked.

"Hopefully soon. I am missing you terribly," Drago replied.

"Me too, darling," Kayla said. "I am leaving in a few days for a photo shoot in Japan. I should be back here in a couple of weeks."

"Okay. Take care, and I will see you soon."

"You do the same," Kayla said. They went dead.

Drago, decide to have a relaxing day and take in the sights. He drove around for a while, then visited the casino and played a few hands of poker.

Later that night, Drago returned to the cottage. He parked his car in the same shady area he used the night before and repeated his movements. The fixer found the hole in the fence. Drago made it big enough for him to go through. It was a tight squeeze. Drago pushed hard and was lucky that his skin-tight suit didn't sustain any damage.

Many of the vehicles that occupied the parking lot the night before were gone, including the one Antoine Bianco had arrived in.

Moving to the rear of the building, Drago noticed the structure was an estate-shaped cottage, completed with many rooms. He discovered another two buildings. The first one he checked and realized it served as the house staff quarters where they would change clothes.

The other one was a garage. Inside were two utility vans. Three boxes occupied the only table in the garage. Drago used the blade from his knife and pried open one of the boxes. Inside, he found many weapons and ammunition. The second box he opened contained hand grenades and a rocket launcher.

The third one had machine guns with plenty

of ammunition, sticks of dynamite, and fuses.

Drago left the garage. He went to the rear of the main cottage. A stone wall flanked the south side of the structure.

There was a door. And a hefty gunner with a weapon slung over his shoulder guarded it.

Drago crouched, roved the ground, and found a handful of gravel. He focuses on a spot well beyond the guard. He threw the small stones.

Predictably, the man left his post to check where the stones had landed. With catlike speed. Drago came up behind and gave the guard a chop to the back of the neck. Knocking him out, and then he dragged the body into the thick bush at the back of the smaller structure.

Drago helped himself to the man's weapon. It was a Lupara; the shotgun favored by many mob families. The Italian mafia were noted for carrying them. Also, the Irish were fond of them as well.

At close range, a Lupara could practically blow a person in two.

Holding the weapon by the barrel, he smashed it against a tree, shattering it into pieces.

Back at the door, it creaked when Drago pulled, and he froze. Hearing nothing, he opened it wide enough to slip into the hallway. Voices came from a room ahead of him.

The fixer hurried forward. The first door was an empty bedroom. On the other side of the hallway was a smaller door. Drago peeked inside the linen closet.

The shelves in the linen closet fill with blankets, sheets, pillowcases, and towels.

At the end of the hallway was another door. The voices were much louder. With back up against the side of the hall, Drago moved closer to the room door.

Drago drew back when he saw how many Irish men were in the room. After not seeing Antoine Bianco among them, Drago decided he had to leave, knowing he had to go past that room to reach the stairs leading to the second floor. He couldn't do that without being seen by someone.

They were too many men in that room to take on, and he wasn't sure his target was still in the building. Drago shook his head in disgust. This assignment wasn't going the way he had hoped it would.

The fixer stayed and listened, hoping he would get information from the man who began to speak.

"My brothers, you will be glad to hear that our mission begins two days from now. The other team members will be here tomorrow. The mission will commence at dawn. We will send the Russians back to Russia. We will also show them the way we do things."

The men applauded when the speaker paused. They hung on to his every word.

"Men, do not become overconfident. The hardest part is ahead of you. Make no mistake. It will be tough, we will cripple them. Our losses so far have been few but very damaging and important to our family."

"It is the price we pay for living high-profile lives and careless with security. And also. The price we pay for getting fat and lazy. It is the price they pay for saying too much at the wrong time, and people. And, having people around them who will sell them out for a price."

The members stayed quiet and looked around at each other.

"Our enemies are like wild dogs. They will attack where there is weakness. That is what happened to our comrades in Jamaica. The Russians saw weakness and took advantage of it."

When the speaker stopped, a young Jamaican pumped a folded fist. "Death to those bastard Russians," he said with a raw Jamaican accent.

"How many more members will be joining us tomorrow?" A man asked.

Drago recognizes the voice to be that of Connor. The Irishman he shot in the leg.

"You are wounded, my brother. I am not sure if you will do much when the time comes to do battle," the speaker said.

**Chapter Six**

Drago had heard enough. He mentally filed the news to relay to Dan McCall later.

It meant that more Irish or Jamaicans were coming to join the group already in the Cayman Islands. They will outnumber the Russians. Out-gunning them might be more difficult.

The Russians so far have been able to bomb the Irish without any problem. Both sides had minor losses before the big battle for the Jamaica turf started. Noel Charles made his deal with James Murphy.

Now Murphy is dead. The question is. "Will the Irish honor the agreement Noel Charles made with James Murphy? Or will they come to a different deal?

Drago thought about this on his way back to the fence without incident and squeezed through the hole. He hurried back to his car and got in. Then he waited as two speeding cars passed before starting the engine.

Back in New York. Dan McCall viewed the footage Drago sent to him in the company of his tech specialist, Mark Glasser.

"Put a name to these faces! And I need them like yesterday, also the license plates on all the vehicles," McCall commanded.

"Will do."

It didn't take the tech long to put names to the faces or ownership of the vehicles.

McCall rejoined Mark Glasser.

"This is what we know so far, sir," Mark explained. " These are the names of the men arriving at the estate building. We have Antoine Bianco, Noel Charles, and Danny O'Brien with an unidentified driver."

"I know about those people," McCall said.

"In the foreground. We have Jack Brennan and Rory Collins."

"Jack Brennan. I heard that name before," McCall stated.

"Yes. You should have. Brennan is on the most wanted list from Interpol."

"And Collins? What do we have on him?"

"Rory Collins also wanted by MI6."

"Any information on their arrival on the Cayman Islands?"

"No flight record for Collins or Brennan."

"Both men hiding somewhere on one of the Islands in South America."

"Why make an appearance now? They must know that one or more agencies will keep tabs on the Russians and Irish battle for Jamaican drug control."

"The conflict is more important than the risk of being seen because there is no extradition from the Island they are living."

"This battle is for the younger members of the family," Mark Glasser said.

"Yes, out in the field. But you need people with experience to plan the attack," McCall said.

"The vehicles. Who owns them?" McCall asked.

"All rentals."

"Get this information back to Drago!" McCall commanded. "Although he knows about Antoine Bianco. And let him know that Joanne is in Barbados on assignment and might come to see him."

Mark Glasser couldn't reach Drago, so he did the next best thing. He relayed the intel through the American Embassy in the Cayman Islands.

Robert Cunningham was the Chargé d'affaires of the American Embassy on the Cayman Islands. You might say that Robert is a citizen of the world. They have stationed his father in many American Embassies around the world.

Cunningham stood six feet five inches. His constant exercising habits gave him a chiseled body.

Robert Cunningham graduated from the Military Academy at West Point, third in his class. He joined the Marines and did two tours in Afghanistan. Robert rose through the ranks in the Marines. He become a Lieutenant Colonel before joining the American Embassy in the Cayman Islands.

The intel from Dan McCall landed on Robert Cunningham's desk.

Joanne McCall. She had worked with Drago on one of his assignments. The two of them had become close and had a brief romantic fling. Joanne, uncle Dan McCall, the boss of the AWB division, had paired her with Drago on her first field operation.

Since that time, she has become a great asset to the company. The worldwide cover for the AWB division was dealers in the textile business.

It has been two years since Drago and Joanne last saw each other. Now, she's on her way from Barbados back to America and decides to stop in the Cayman Islands to visit Drago.

At the hotel, Drago checked with the night clerk for any messages. There were none.

In his suite, after a change of clothes. Drago poured a glass of Jack Daniels from the mini-bar and sipped it.

He thought about the events that had

happened earlier at the Irishmen's hideout. Drago again viewed the footage he had taken of the people and vehicles.

Vaguely, he heard a knock on the door between the two suites.

"It's open," he said without moving from his position.

The connecting doors open and close.

"Hey you," the voice said.

Drago looked up. Joanne stood in the doorway. She wore something blue and light that hid nothing beneath it.

"Sit down!"

She sat down beside him and crossed her legs. The blue item slit up to her hip, and a part fell to the floor.

Joanne rests her head on Drago's shoulder.

"How are you, Rick?" she asked, kissing him on the cheeks.

"I am okay."

"I miss you terribly. Do you miss me?"

"If I say no, I'll be lying. You know how this works. We can't get too emotionally attached working in the field."

"I know. There's nothing wrong with comforting each other now and then."

"Is this what this is? You come to comfort me?" he asked.

"Yes. If you let me."

"Uh."

"You look tired," she said.

"I am. Just return from an encounter with the Irish mob," Drago replied.

Joanne got up. She took him by the hand and led him to the bed. With a loving shove, Drago fell back on the bed.

She hastily removed his trousers and shirt.

"Let me take care of you," she said.

She smiled and moved between his legs. Joanne moved her fingers over his chest.

"Too tired."

"Just relaxed," she said.

"What did you have in mind?"

Joanne kissed him, her mouth closing over his with a sultry suction, the warm length of her body pressing against him, probing his lips with her tongue. Drago moved his hands to the opening of her dress, feeling the velvety muscles and smooth body as she leaned into him.

He shifted a little, bringing her down beside him on the bed. Drago moved his fingers and found her left breast with a hardened nipple. She broke away from him and stood up. With a deft movement, she shrugged the garment off her shoulders.

She wore nothing underneath, and her breasts tumbled out with enormous hard nipples.

Joanne stepped out of the garment as it fell

to the carpet. She picked it up and tossed it onto a chair, then murmured. "You're not too tired to have me now. Are you?"

"Damn, Joanne, you know I can't refuse."

"Then take me now!" She pulled his hands to her breasts. Her mouth was wet as she whispered in his ear. "Hard, harder." She took up a compulsive rhythm as she lay underneath him.

Someone tapped on the door. "Who is it?" the fixer asked.

"Robert Cunningham."

Drago shook Joanne. She awakened immediately, eyes fixed on him with awareness. She looked across the room, then smiled. "Good morning," Joanne said.

"Someone's at the door."

"Who is it?"

"Someone from the Embassy. Robert Cunningham."

"You met him before?"

"No."

Joanne swung her legs to the carpet and went through the connecting door to her suite. The fixer heard the familiar morning routine, clearing the throat and the gargling.

Drago got up, walked to the door, and opened it. The man stepped into the suite.

"Morning," he said to Drago.

Cunningham opened his attaché case and handed a sealed envelope to the fixer.

"This came in for you early this morning," Cunningham said.

Drago opened the envelope. He looked at the photos and read the information attached to each person's face. Another document informs him of a Russian fishing trawler anchored off the coast of Jamaica.

"Joanne McCall arrived on the Island last night. Have you seen her?" Robert asked.

"Yes. I have," the fixer muttered.

Drago set the envelope aside, got up, and headed for the bathroom.

"Will she be assisting you with this assignment?" Cunningham asked.

The fixer didn't answer.

"What do you know about this Russian trawler anchor off the coast of Jamaica?"

Robert flipped open a notepad.

"The latest from them was engine trouble. They are waiting for a replacement part to arrive." Cunningham continued. "A mate and three deckhands came ashore to wait for and take the replacement part back to the trawler."

"Broken engine, my ass. Did you run a check on ownership of the vessel?"

"Yes. We did."

"And?"

"The vessel is owned by a Ukrainian business person named Oleg Popov. He was a lieutenant. KGB, first Directorate. According to his file, three years ago, he went into the fishing business in partnership with a member of the oligarchs. Oleg Popov now lives in Koncha-Zaspa, one of many interesting neighborhoods in the Ukraine."

"What about the partner?" Drago asked.

"Lev Ivanov was born into wealth. He is a bit of a womanizer. Word is. Ivanov never travels alone, always in the company of his bodyguards. I might add, who are all women?"

"Lucky fellow," Drago said.

Cunningham continues. "His father became rich doing business on the black market. Now, the son has his hands in everything, from drugs, weapons, and smuggling. You name it, he's into it."

"Any information on the captain or the crew on board the trawler?"

"Yes. Only the Captain. His name's Andrei Volkov, a veteran of the sea. Andrei Volkov, began drinking heavily after his wife died, and lost his captain's rank for huge cargo vessels," Cunningham explained.

" Not much to go on. The crew could be there to take on the Irish mob," Drago muttered. "What about the members of the crew that went ashore? Are they still accounted for?"

"They stayed ashore until the engine part was ready to be transported back to the trawler."

"So."

"I am not up to date with this operation. What do we expect to gain from the outcome of this?"

"Only McCall can give you the answer to your question," Drago stated.

The fixer knew that AWB operations were beyond Cunningham's pay grade.

"Uh, oh, I see," Cunningham said, with disappointment in his tone of voice.

"Will you be returning to your office later today?"

"Yes. In the afternoon. Is there something you need?"

"No. Nothing at the moment."

A knock on the door.

"It's open. Come in!"

Joanne opened the door and entered the suite. "Good morning," she said. "Thought I heard voices."

"Good morning to you," Drago said. "This is Robert Cunningham."

Joanne extended a hand, and Cunningham took it. "Good morning to you also," he said.

"Hope I am not intruding," Joanne said.

"No. I am about to leave," Cunningham said.

"It was nice to meet you."

"Same here," Cunningham replied.

The fixer got up and walked with Cunningham to the door.

"Goodbye, Drago."

"See you," Drago stated and closed the door.

"So. Why was Robert here?" Joanne asked.

"Cunningham brought a report from your uncle."

"What about?"

"It's on the table. You can read it," Drago said. "That was smooth, knocking on the door."

"Yes. I thought it was," Joanne said. "I am not all beauty you now."

Drago chuckled. "Don't remind me!"

## Chapter Seven

Joanne took up the file and read it.

"I am about to order breakfast. What do you want?" Drago asked.

"I'd like melba toast with jam, orange juice, and expresso," Joanne replied.

After they ate breakfast, Drago asked, "What do you think about the information in the file?"

"The black guy looks familiar."

"His name's Noel Charles. He is a Jamaican," Drago said. "Have you ever visited Jamaica?"

"No."

"When are you planning to leave?"

"Don't you want me to stay and give you a hand?" Joanne asked. "I'm not in a rush."

"You should inform your uncle of your plans!" Drago advised.

"I will call him later."

"Just out of curiosity," Drago said, "how did you know I was here on assignment?"

"Simple," Joanne said. "Who is your target?"

Drago pointed to the photo of Antoine Bianco. "This man is a contract killer. I must admit, he is one of the best. Every law enforcement agency wants to get their hands on him. We were asked to save the taxpayer's money and put him down."

"Where is Bianco now?"

"I don't know. And Antoine has not surfaced after I took this picture of him at the cottage rented by the Irish."

"The Irish mob hired him for this rumble with the Russians. It must be important for them to pay the fees he charges."

"I believe it is more than the control of drugs from Jamaica," Drago suggested.

"So. Bianco's gone into hiding."

"Antoine may be here for a specific target. He might not be involved with the gang's battle."

"Do you have any idea who the target might be?" Joanne asked.

"It could be a member of the Russian oligarch. or a relative of the inner circle."

"What are your plans?"

"Only one thing I am interested in."

"What's that?"

"Elliminating Antoine Bianco."

Joanne took the file and studied the photos of the people, then placed it back on the table.

"Later today, I will return to the cottage that the Irish team has rented and do more scouting of the structure's back entrance," Drago stated.

"I am coming with you."

"Somehow, I knew you were going to say that."

"I am going for a swim," Joanne said. "You coming?"

"No. You go ahead. I'll see you when you get back."

Joanne got up from the table and went to her suite. A few moments later, she returned to Drago's suite wearing a Flounce Tropical Print one-piece v-neck swimwear.

"You like?" Joanne asked Drago while turning around and giving him the full view of her cleavage.

The fixer smiled.

Joanne gave Drago a tender kiss on the

forehead and went through the door.

Drago dressed in a short white trousers, a multi-color short-sleeved shirt, and white sandals, with a beach towel over his shoulder, and took the stairs down to the first landing.

The fixer got into his rental vehicle, tossed the towel on the back seat, and drove the twenty-minute journey to the Irishmen's cottage. He parked the car and followed the public access path between the trees leading to the beach.

Drago walked along the beach. He couldn't reach the back of the cottage from the beach. The Irishmen were careful in choosing this cottage with no access to the water.

At the back were ten-foot-high cliffs covered in vines and jagged edges on the rocks by years of the salted sea water beating against them.

A cool breeze from far out on the sea hit Drago on his face and caused the water to form caps and foam.

He was approaching the cottage from the east side. No guards were visible. The Irish didn't think it necessary to post guards because of the jagged, slippery, and high rocks protecting the back of the structure.

Many people were on the beach. Some were taking in the rays of the sun. They were people waterskiing, sail-boating, and snorkeling.

Children were building sand castles. Other

people played in the surf as it rolled ashore, gathering the seashells from the sand.

Drago had seen enough.

Back at the hotel, Joanne called her uncle Dan McCall on his private line.

"Yes," McCall said, answering the call on the second buzz.

"Hello. Sir," Joanne stated.

"Have you spoken with Drago?"

"Yes. I saw Drago earlier today."

"And?"

"He said I should clear it with you before deciding to stay here," Joanne said.

"Did Drago ask you to stay and help him?"

"Not in so many words. But I know Rick would like me to stay."

"Where is he now?"

"Drago went to scout the rear of the cottage and check on his target."

"Okay."

"Well. Should I stay here and give Drago a hand?"

"Only if he asked," McCall advised.

"Thanks."

"Your mother asked when will you be coming home."

"I will call her after speaking with Rick about staying."

Joanne was going to stay. She had decided

Sherwin A. Goodman

not to leave until after the assignment was complete.

Drago returned to the hotel, and later that night, he took the hardware he would need and put it in the trunk of his rental car.

In Jamaica, the Russian Trawler lifted the anchor and moved further offshore on the north side of the Island. At six thirty pm, a rubber craft lowered over the port side, and twelve heavily armed men dressed in wet suits. They got on board the rubber craft and then headed for the shore.

The squad leader was a retired member of Russia's elite forces. His name. Olaf Krinsenko. He was the head of security for Lev Ivanov's dad. Now, he trains the women who protect the son. A shattered left leg caused his retirement from the Russian military.

After retiring. Krinsenko started his security firm and worked for many of Russia's oligarchs and other important officials. Now, he is here, leading a squad of armed men on the assault upon the Jamaican and Irish mob. The target was a warehouse near the seaport.

The Port of Ocho Rios is on the north side of the Island. Rios is one of the busiest ports on the Island. It is about 60 kilometers from Kingston and about 90 kilometers east of Montego Bay.

At 4 a.m., Drago and Joanne entered

Drago's rental and headed to the cottage where the Irishmen were staying.

The vans roared to life when Drago and Joanne reached the gate. Seeing that the cottage parking area was now empty of cars, and the only vehicles were the two vans. Drago had to make a quick decision and pick one van. He chooses the last one to leave the cottage. The driver was black, wearing a leather jacket and a Jamaican cricket cap. Loud reggae music came from the inside of the vehicle. The man was moving his head from side to side and singing the words to the song that was playing.

The first van turned left, heading towards the direction that Drago thought it would, but the van in which Drago had hitched his ride turned and headed right.

Leaving Joanne with the car, the van wasn't moving fast. Drago seized the moment and darted to the rear of the moving van. He jumped onto the bumper and used the rack on the roof to steady himself.

Drago used the rack on the roof to pull himself up, then lay flat as the driver increased his speed.

It was now so early that traffic was sparse. And fewer pedestrians were out and about.

The van had covered four blocks when the driver slowed and turned off the main street onto an unpaved gravel road.

Drago spotted a sign on a piece of wood nailed to a tree that read. "Private Property. No persons allowed."

To Drago's surprise, the driver ignored the posted signs and continued driving. A couple of minutes after passing the last posted sign, the vehicle slowed down as the driver maneuvered between the trees and stopped.

Drago got out of the vehicle when it slowed down in the same way he had got on. Using one of the many large trees, he hid and watched as the van came to a halt. But the driver never came out. Drago waited, then saw a device going up through the roof. He assumed it was a jamming device the Irishmen were using to jam any signals the Russians would try to send out.

Drago's watch told him it was five-thirty in the morning. He remembered that the attack would begin at six am.

"If the jamming device was in range. Then the place where the Russians are staying has to be close."Drago thought to himself.

"And where was Joanne?"

Joanne followed the other van to its destination. She stayed within sight of the vehicle and was not too close to arousing any suspicion from the occupants. When the van stopped and parked, she watched as the squad, dressed in camouflage suits and fully armed, got out one after the other. The moonlight was going dim. Joanne looked at her watch. The time was five forty-five am.

Joanne found the public parking area with access to the beach. She parked the car, popped the trunk, got herself combat-ready, and then walked along the beach in the direction the vehicle had come to a stop.

It appears that the Irishmen had picked the perfect morning for the assault on the Russians. It would be a humid day as dark clouds filled the early morning skies.

The rain was up there, and it was going to fall. Maybe the rain will come this morning, afternoon, or evening.

The morning wind was brisk, coming in over the ocean from the northwest side of the Island. Small waves formed with white foam on the tops and rolled ashore. The sound of gunfire caused the birds in the trees to scatter.

Joanne broke into a stride, nearing the beach cottage where the Russians were. Joanne got down on her stomach and used the sand banks to get a closer look at the gunfight.

Drago didn't have to wait. The sound of an automatic gun broke the morning silence. Sprinting toward the sound, he came to a broken-down fence and went through it.

A member of the Irish squad saw him, but thought he was a fellow member of the Jamaican team, the way he looked in the early morning under dark skies.

The Fixer triggered the LCR 38.5p, driving the man to the ground with a hole in his chest.

Drago has a habit of not wasting good ammo. He puts away the LCR 38 for the machine gun lying beside the dead man, then he frisks the man's pockets for more ammunition and turns up five magazines for the machine gun.

The battle raged on as the Russian squad was making a stand. Dark clouds in the sky gave Drago the perfect cover, allowing him to get close to the action.

The Fixer was hunting for one man, and if he had to go through the Irish hit-men, he would do that to get the job done.

Drago had seen the beach cottage on the other side of the structure.

From where he was at the moment, the building was larger.

The Irishmen had lost the element of surprise, but they weren't about to quit, as the Russians were ready and waiting.

**Chapter Eight**

The Irishman weaved around the north side
of the building as the Jamaican team laid down,

suppressing cover fire.

An explosion occurred from the opposite side of the cottage. Two of the Russian Range Rover went up in smoke.

Drago kept looking, hoping to finish his assignment by taking out Antoine Bianco. He wanted to follow the Irish triggermen, but two of their squad stood in his path.

Drago moved towards the men, but suddenly, he had to take cover as the Russian gunners sent a swarm of bullets toward the Irish triggermen; he hit the ground and rolled behind one of the palm trees.

The Russians spotted Drago, then made him the target and opened fire, pinning him down behind the tree.

The gunman stopped firing. Drago made a break from behind the tree, placing his back against the building, and made his way closer to the window the gunmen used.

Drago believed the shooter was replacing the empty clip with another full clip of ammo. Using the machine gun he had taken from the dead soldier earlier, Drago sprayed the window with a swarm of bullets.

Rounds punched through the badly damaged wooden frame of the window, drilling the man in the head and chest as bullets from the machine gun made the man's body jump around before going limp.

The upper part of the shooter's body fell forward through the window.

Drago returned his attention to where the Irishman was standing before the Russian opened fire.

The two Irish gunners were gone from their position. The Fixer heard yells and orders given in Russian by someone in charge, and a utility van parked in the courtyard exploded in flames.

Neither the Russians nor the Irishmen would leave anyone alive unless they needed information. A utility van exploded, killing gunners from the Irish squad.

The foyer leading to the north side of the house was a shamble caused by the exploding van. Two dead Jamaicans lay sprawled on the ground, another blocking the side door.

Drago hurried on as the Irish squad was moving deeper into the house. Dead bodies littered the floor.

The Fixer stopped at the corner of a room. From the corner of his right eye, he saw a figure coming in through the shattered window.

"Hi," Joanne said, standing behind Drago.

"I was wondering where you were."

"How is it going?"

"Not sure."

"Any sign of your target?"

"Nothing, damn. I hate to think it, but Antoine Bianco might not be here."

"No intel on him?"

"Nothing in the last intel delivered by Robert Cunningham."

Moving from their position, Drago and Joanne slowly walked to the mahogany staircase leading to the upstairs rooms.

Two bodies tumble down the stairs and land on the floor. Drago and Joanne drew back. They were fair game from both sides, the Russians from above and the Irish squad trying to gain access to the stairs, and couldn't take on the two teams of killers all at once.

Drago's priority was to eliminate Antoine Bianco. Joanne moved back to the room she had entered through the window. A gunner was trying to use the same routine. Joanne squeezed off a round, and the bullet found its mark in the center of the Gunner's forehead. The force of the bullet jerked the man's head as his body slid backward. The man was dead before the body hit the ground.

Drago continued past the stairs. He came to the kitchen, and more bodies slumped on the table, still in the sitting position.

A quick search of the dead men revealed no information about who they were. Shadowy figures went past the kitchen window.

The sun had begun rising in a blood-red color. Time was getting short for the Fixer to find his target and complete his mission.

Not knowing who the figures were, he moved swiftly behind them. Drago would engage with anyone in his way.

Using the LCF.38sp with a silencer attached, he fired three kill shots, then stepped over the fallen bodies, holding the gun with both hands at shoulder level. Drago moved forward, continuously checking from left to right and overhead for any movement.

The Irish hit squad had gained access to the second floor and continued to batter the Russians.

Joanne got herself caught up in the crossfire between the two hit squads.

Her presence confused the gunners for a while until one of them opened fire at her. With bullets hitting the ground at her feet, Joanne took cover behind one of the damaged utility vans.

Returning fire, she took out two of the men. Joanne wasn't sure if the men were Irish or Russians. To her, it didn't matter,

Moments later, Drago reached the area and saw that Joanne was pinned down behind the van. Using hand gestures, Drago and Joanne attack the position of the two hit squads.

Sherwin A. Goodman

## *Jamaica*

Back in Jamaica. Noel Charles had moved his operation from the warehouse. Noel stored the cargo in two rented cast containers, then moved them by truck to a vacant land lot before leaving Jamaica with the Irish squad to the Cayman Islands.

Charles left behind his posse, second in command, to take care of the cargo should anything arise.

Levi Butcher grew up on the streets of Harbor View, where crime was the only way to survive. Dealing with drugs, street corner purse snatching, looting rum shops, and other establishments.

After Levi Butcher's mother died of an overdose, his grandparents took on the responsibility of raising him. Then, his father moved away and married another woman. Levi Butcher's grandparents tried to give him a good life by sending him to learn a trade in motor mechanics. He would attend the trade school during the day, but at night, Levi was on the street corners selling drugs.

The money from the drug selling was way better than what he was earning at the mechanic trade. After meeting the boss, Levi decide to become a full-time drug dealer and quickly caught the attention of Noel Charles, who promoted him to the number two position in the posse.

Levi Butcher sits in his dark blue BMW, parked between the two cast containers with the drug cargo inside, and at the back of the BMW was a black GMC SUV with tinted windows parked, with five other members of the gang sitting inside facing the other direction.

They were to protect the cargo until they shipped it to the rightful buyers.

In New York, Dan McCall entered his office at seven am. On his desk was a memo McCall picked it up and read.

(Lev Ivano is due to arrive in the Cayman Islands at seven am)

McCall's secretary, Dorothy Adams, enters McCall's office carrying a cup of coffee.

"Morning, Sir," Dorothy said.

"Good morning."

"That memo came in a few minutes ago."

"Where is Drago?"

"He is still in the Cayman Islands, was the last report."

"Get in touch with him!" McCall commanded. "Why was Ivano going to the Cayman Islands by plane instead of using his super-powered yacht," McCall thought.

Moments later, McCall's secretary reentered

his office. "Drago, can't be reached," she said."

"What do you mean, he can't be reached?"

"That's what Glasser said."

McCall left his office with Dorothy in tow and went to see Glasser. "What are you saying, Drago? Is he unreachable?" McCall growled.

"I tried his cell and got no reply," Mark Glasser replied.

"Do what you have to do, but get him! He has to know about the member of the Russian Oligarch in the Cayman Islands as we speak."

"Working on it," Glasser said.

"When you reach him, send this message urgently, and also see that our office in the Caymans gets a copy."

Levi stationed two other members at the warehouse. The men sat in a BMW SUV out of view from anyone going to the warehouse. But in a place where they could see who approached the building.

One man was Marvin Campbell. He and Noel Charles grew up on the streets and also started selling drugs at an early age. The other lookout member was a cousin of Marvin. His name was Victor Campbell. Like Marvin, he was also a long-time member of the gang.

At midnight, two black sedans pulled up at the front of the warehouse.

A member of the lookout posse put through

a call to

Levi Butcher.

"We have visitors."

"How many?" Levi asked.

"Two vehicles, no one has gotten out yet," the caller said.

"Okay, we are on our way, and if they try to leave, delay them!" The line went dead.

One vehicle had the lights off and crawled to the south side of the warehouse.

Four men exited the sedan parked at the front of the building, all of them wearing dark clothing and armed with automatic weapons, and approached the door of the warehouse.

Cutting torches were used to remove the steel bars and bolts, giving the teams access to the inside of the structure. Both teams used precision timing and entered at the same time.

Levi Butcher and his crew arrived seconds after the Russian squad entered the warehouse.

This crew was the elite of the posse. The members Noel Charles took to the Cayman Islands were all new members and left the hardcore, more skilled guys in Jamaica with Levi to protect the cargo.

Only one road leads to and from the warehouse. Levi had unhitched the cast container from one truck and brought the vehicle along to block the entrance to the warehouse.

They armed every one of the squad members with a Uzi gun and carrying a machete stuck under the belt around their waist.

Behind the building was a gully, bushy fern vines, and many large jagged rocks and trees.

Knowing the area, Levi knew that the only passage from the warehouse was on the road where he had the truck blocking the entrance.

The team emerged from the vehicle and began walking to the building.

Shoulder to shoulder, the men walked holding the guns at waist height, the left hand supporting the weapon and the right hand ready on the trigger.

Now. The two men lookout team left the SUV and moved closer to the building.

"Can you see the visitors?" Levi asked.

"No. The visitors broke into the warehouse," Marvin replied.

Marvin and his Cousin Victor reached the side of the building where one vehicle was parked. First, the two men used their machetes and slashed the four tires. Then Marvin shattered the windshield and the back glass.

Levi and his crew rendered the vehicle parked at the front of the warehouse helpless. Tires slashed. Levi and his crew also damaged the front and rear lights.

Inside the warehouse, the only items were a

few tables and chairs scattered about the area.

The air conditioning units were also in the warehouse, there was an office with a filing cabinet and other sections divided by thick plastic hanging from the rafters to the floor.

By the time the Russians realize that something is wrong, the door to the front of the warehouse opens, and four men come in armed with Uzis and machetes.

Two of the Russians tried to exit the building through the side door but had to retreat inside when Marvin and Victor started shooting at them.

Levi and his team began the assault on the Russian after hearing the sounds of gunfire from the outside. Levi knew that Marvin and Victor were positioned to stop anyone from escaping.

The Russian squad turned over a few tables, using them to shelter themselves from the onslaught of bullets coming from the posse.

Return fire. The bullets found the targets of two members from the posse squad were hit in their legs and shoulders.

It didn't take long for the posse to subdue the Russian squad. Five of the members were dead. The last one surrendered after sustaining bullet wounds to his hip and chest.

Levi then had his team drive the two Russian vehicles with the flat tires into the warehouse, away from prying eyes until they decided what to do with them.

They tortured information out of the only Russian still alive before shooting him in the forehead.

The posse then carted the bodies of the Russians deep into the bushy area at the back of the warehouse and placed them in a shallow grave.

Levi also learned that many Russians had arrived on a fishing trawler owned by a member of the Russian Oligarch and that they anchored the boat outside the coastline of Jamaica, waiting for them to return before heading back to Russia.

Lev Ivano. The owner of the trawler and a high-ranked member of the Oligarch were to arrive in the Cayman Islands that same day.

At six am, a private jet with Lev Ivano and his entourage on board touches down on The General Aviation Terminal (GAT) private airstrip.

Then, at precisely seven minutes after six, as Ivano followed the last bodyguard on to the first landing, a shot rang out from a far away.

The bullet found its mark in the center of Ivano's forehead. Two of the bodyguards took Ivano back into the plane, and the other bodyguards on the tarmac drew their weapons and began looking around, trying to figure out where the shot had come from.

The flight attendants, pilots, and bodyguards worked on Ivano's body, trying to revive him until they realized that his body was lifeless.

Panic set in among the crew.

What will they do with the body of an elite member of the Oligarch? The head of Ivano's security, decide to call the cottage, knowing that the leader is an ex-military man and might give him advice on what to do with Ivano's body.

Sherwin A. Goodman

# Chapter Nine

The call was unsuccessful because the Irish squad had jammed all signals going out and coming into the cottage by mobile phones.

On the roof of a building, a lone figure got up from lying on his stomach, removed the silencer, the stand, and the scope from the long-range rifle, put the pieces into a backpack, and left the building.

Once again, Antoine Bianco successfully carried out his assignment. He then drove the rental vehicle to the house where the Irish squad rented and left the gun and the car there.

Antoine Bianco then took a taxi to the airport and caught Delta Airlines' first flight to Miami, Florida.

The gunfight between the two squads was coming to a close, as the sounds of bullets were not steady. In the distance, the sound of approaching law enforcement officers.

"Let's get out of here," Drago said to Joanne.

"Aren't you going to see if the target is here?"

"No time, and we're not sure who is still alive in the house."

"Okay, let's go," Joanne said.

"Where did you park?" Drago asked.

"Follow me!"

Murky shadows mired to the left of the Fixer and Joanne as they prepared to go to the vehicles. Drago wasn't worried about them. The shadows turned out to be members of the Jamaican posse. The gunners seemed wary as a wolf, slowly advancing away from the dying sound of gunfire.

Drago and the two men exchanged glances briefly. The gunners said something to each other as Drago and Joanne disappeared from view.

*New York, New York.*

There were days when Dan McCall would give anything for a few hours of interruption in his office. Today is one of those days.

Since early morning, Dan McCall was sitting at his desk, going over the latest intel. Part of the time, he was in the technology room with Mark Glasser, trying to understand why the agent couldn't reach Rick Drago.

The intel from the Cayman Islands was not surprising to the boss of the AWB department.

"Lev Ivanov, a prominent member of the Russian Oligarch, was shot and killed in the early morning hours on the Cayman Islands as he was about to embark from his private jet. No arrest for the shooting and the police have no leads."

Taking a break from reading the intel printouts, Dan sipped on the cup of coffee. Then, his secretary Dorothy peeks into the office.

"Drago is on the phone," Dorothy said.

Dan picked up the receiver. "What's going on?" Dan asked.

"The assets weren't in play," Drago said.

"I know. That's because Antoine Bianco was at a private airstrip on the Cayman Islands shooting a member of the Russian Oligrath, Lev Ivano."

"What time did that happen?"

"Moments after the private jet landed, the time was around seven am."

"Any intel on Antoine?"

"Nothing at the moment, but we are working on it."

"Antoine would have left the Island soon after the shooting if it was him," Drago said.

"Stay there until I contact you. Do a little sightseeing and R& R!'

In Arizona. A long way from the fighting in the Cayman Islands. A high-ranked member of the Irish mob and his bodyguards were gunned down when a pair of motorcycle teams rode up on them and opened fire as they sat eating brunch at a restaurant owned by the Irish family.

In New Mexico. They bombed a brothel owned by a member of the Russian mob. Ten women perished, and it hurt a dozen more in the blast. Many clienteles in the establishment at the time of the blasts, was also hurt. Some were in critical condition, and others had minor injuries. They took all of them to the hospital for treatment.

The good thing about what was happening in Arizona and New Mexico. The FBI, Home Security, and the DEA were all doing their part to put an end to the situation and stop the bloodbath.

Antoine Bianco was Dan McCall's problem. His number one agent was on the case, but Antoine Bianco was slippery as a grease monkey.

Dan McCall continued looking for a connection between what was happening on the Cayman Islands and the shooting in Arizona and the bombing in New Mexico.

The phone on McCall's desk buzzed. Dan picked up the receiver.

"Yes," McCall said.

"Drago is on the phone," Dorothy said.

"Tell him to hang up and call back on the secure line!" McCall ordered.

Moments later, the green phone on McCall's desk buzzed.

McCall picked up the receiver. "Rick, I need you to come in."

"What's up?"

"I'll explain when you get here."

"What about Diana?"

"I thought she had already left."

"No. Diana is still here."

"I don't know what to say to the two of you. How soon can you get here?"

"Will be on the first available flight from here to the USA."

"Let me know when you have the flight information."

"Will do," Drago replied. Then the phone went dead as McCall hung up.

McCall buzzed his secretary, Dorothy.

"Yes," Dorothy said, pushing the reply button.

"What's the latest on Antoine Bianco?" McCall asked.

"Antoine got off the Delta flight and

checked into the Mandarin Oriental Hotel," Dorothy said.

"Is he still there?"

"Antoine has not checked out."

"Book a room for Drago at the Mandarin Oriental!" McCall ordered.

McCall's problem was with Antoine Bianco. The man never stayed in any place for very long.

Unlike a team or a squad, Antoine had no known associates who could betray him, making him a hard target.

The man was as slippery as a snake covered in oil. Getting Bianco was like trying to capture a ghost.

McCall looked at the time displayed on the clock sitting on his desk. Drago will be here soon, and hopefully, he can get to Florida and eliminate Antoine Bianco before he slips away.

The bombing in New Mexico had started a war between the Irish and the Russians.

They hurt innocent bystanders when the Bank at a local strip mall was robbed, and they exchanged gunfire between the police and the robbers. The Bank was under investigation by the feds for money laundering for the Russian Mafia.

Civilians had no business getting hurt in these gang wars. Being in the wrong place at the wrong time can't be helped, and innocent people getting hurt are looked upon as collateral damage.

Now, fighting between the two families was happening in different parts of the world, the Cayman Islands and New Mexico.

As McCall read the latest reports on the conflict. "This has to be more than the control of drugs coming out of Jamaica," he thought to himself.

Nothing new came in about the drive-by shooting in Arizona. The local police were still searching for the shooters.

This conflict between the Irish and the Russians reminded the AWB top man of similar wars between the different families of the Mafia. It was rare that innocent civilians ever get hurt when the Italian Mafia go to war with each other. Women and children have always sheltered away from the battle.

The Russians started this war when they tried to muscle their way into the Jamaican drug trade. Not knowing about the close relationship the head of the Jamaican trade has with James Murphy, the Irish businessperson on the Island.

The Fixer was treating himself to a cup of coffee given to him by McCall's secretary Dorothy when Dan entered the office and sank down into a chair behind the desk.

"I don't know what to say," Drago

quipped."But you look unkept."

McCall cracked a smile. "Why do you think that is? I have no down time these last few days. Reports after reports arrived in the last forty eight hours."

"So what's the latest?" Drago inquired, and took a sip of coffee.

"Where do I begin. These reports are not your concern. You have your orders to eliminate Antoine Bianco, and the latest on him is Florida. That's where you are going."

"Let's talk about The Enforcer," Drago suggest.

"Glad you brought that up," McCall said, as he began to flip through the sheets of paper on his desk.

"What are you looking for?"

"Do you know that Antoine Bianco have a older brother?"

"No. Don't tell me that he's in the same line of work?"

"Ah, here it is," McCall said handing a sheet of paper with a picture on it across the desk to Drago.

"Tito Bianco," Drago said.

"Got this. He is a Merc: Currently in Eastern Europe."

"How good is this intel?"

"It's from Interpol. We have to treat it as

legit."

"Do they know each other?"

"Information is as follows. Tito knows about Antoine, but, Antoine do not know anything about his older brother, because Tito has a different mother."

"Older. You said Tito is older."

"Yes. Four year older."

"Both are in the business of gun for hire."

"Yes. It appears that way," McCall concluded.

"Family business," Drago stated.

"There is no confirm amount of killings credited to Tito. Unlike Antoine. Interpol attribute more than a dozen deaths to him, but they were never able to prove a single one. He's slick and vicious."

"The same thing for the FBI," Drago said.

McCall went on. "According to information received. A few months ago Tito himself vanished. No one had any idea where he was until he turned up at a private clinic in Ghana for treatment to multiple gunshot wounds."

Drago finished the coffee and put the empty cup on the corner of the table in front of him.

McCall reached into the top drawer of his desk and produced an airline ticket. "First-class. From our taxpayers."

Drago accepted it. He was booked on an

evening flight out of LaGuardia Airport.

*Florida*

Rick Drago arrived in Florida and checked into The Mandarin Oriental Hotel. Drago's suite was across the hall from where Antoine Bianco was staying.

Not wanting to be nosey, Drago started a conversation with the lift operator and smartly asked about the guests staying on the floor.

According to the operator, the guest in suite 1707 across the hall from 1708, where Drago staying, hasn't been seen since he checked into the Hotel.

That information did not surprise Drago. The Enforcer was known for not staying in a place for any length of time.

Drago knew he had to get into suite 1707 and check for any clues to where Antoine Bianco was, or where he disappeared before reporting back to McCall.

At 2300 that night, Rick Drago entered suite 1707 after picking the door lock. His search of the room didn't provide any information about Antoine Bianco.

Nothing in the suite was disturbed.

Towels were never used, and the minibar was still fully stocked.

It appeared Bianco never stayed in the suite after the Hotel staff prepared it.

At seven am, Drago contacted McCall and brought him up to date with what he found out about Antoine Bianco.

"Morning, Rick," McCall said.

"Here was a dead end," Drago stated.

"Yes. I know," McCall replied.

"What's next?"

"You are booked on the American Airlines flight to the Dominican Republic leaving Miami at noon today."

"Okay. What's there?"

"Antoine Bianco flew from Miami, Florida, to The Dominican Republic the same day he checked into the hotel."

"Where am I going to find him when I get there?"

"We are working on it as we speak."

Minutes later, Drago checked out of the Mandarin Oriental hotel and went to the Miami airport for his flight to The Dominican Republic.

*Dominican Republic*

It looked like another house in the upscale neighborhood of Bavaro, located in the Province of La Altagracia. The house was two stories high and had a manicured lawn and a midsize swimming pool.

The neighbors had heard that the latest owner was an old English man living somewhere in the United Kingdom.

Many of the neighbors were more than curious when they saw a rented SUV parked in the driveway, and a tall, muscular young man got out carrying a suit bag over his shoulder and entered the house.

No one in the neighborhood has ever seen the new owner. A lawyer acting on behalf of the buyer purchased the house.

After the previous owner passed away, leaving the property to his grandson, the young man immediately put the structure up for sale.

Gossip started again amongst the neighbors who the mystery man was. Some say that the man was a relative of the owner. The man didn't look like the type of person on a vacation trip to the Island.

Most visitors carry more than one piece of luggage. If anyone had got up the nerve to go and welcome the man to the neighborhood, they would have rudely turned away.

## Chapter Ten

Antoine Bianco never like to be disturbed by anyone except his business associates. And he never accepts friendship from anyone except of his choosing, which was few.

This building will serve as a safe house for the Irish members needing a place to lie low. Antoine Bianco (The Enforcer) was the first to use it. He could unwind and probably have a little fun here on the Island. Bianco felt safe. Who would look for a hit-man in a beautiful place like this? Interpol, CIA, or any other law enforcement agency.

Antoine was to stay on the Island until he made contact about his next job for the Irish mob.

An hour after Antoine Bianco entered the house, a catering van pulled into the driveway and unloaded what looked like food.

A nosey stay-at-home parent took notes of the items carted into the house, then notified her friends that the man was stocking up on food and drinks. Suggesting he could be planning a party.

After signing for the delivery, The Enforcer tried to remember the last time he went to a classy restaurant and enjoyed a meal in the company of a woman.

As for women, the only women he had in his company for the last few years were provided through his associates, and they were either strippers or prostitutes.

In his profession, The Enforcer never wanted to be close to any female, knowing that moment he could be away from them.

His father (Victor Bianco) was taken away from him at a young age before his very eyes. Antoine remembers going with his dad to collect his winnings from the bookie. The numbers that his dad played every week had finally paid off. On the way home, two men got out of a car and gave his dad a beating. Victor Bianco fought back. But he was no match for the two goons. Antoine was helpless. After the beating, the men took the thousand dollars from him, got back into the car, and drove away.

Rumors surface as people pointed the finger at the bookie. Many people believed the bookie (Robert Brentwood)didn't like to paying out such large amounts of cash and set up the robbery.

Antoine's father never recovered from that beating. He died two weeks later from the beating. The Enforcer was only twelve years old at the time of his dad's death, but he remembered the faces of the men and secretly vowed to have his revenge one day.

That day came five years later. The Enforcer started his first job as a delivery boy for a grocery store. It turned out that his first delivery was to the place his father had visited on the fatal day five years ago.

Upon entering the establishment, Antoine called out the name written on the bill that was attached to the paper bag. The order was for two bottles of salted peanuts.

Most of the tables were occupied. Hearing

the name, a man at a corner table raised his hand. As Antoine walked to the man, two tables to the right, he saw the two men who had beaten his father sitting in the company of another man.

"Phone call for you, boss," the man behind the counter shouted.

Antoine looked and saw the third man sitting at the table, got up, and took the phone.

The Enforcer would remember the face of the third person responsible for the death of his father.

Days turned into weeks as Antoine studied the habits of the three men. Where they went, how long they stayed, and the women they spent time with outside.

Home addresses of their women. The cars they drive, and the visits to the hair salon.

Victor Bianco kept a gun wrapped in a towel hidden away in a gym bag. Antoine uses his father's gun to settle the score with his killers. He cleaned and oiled the gun, making sure that it worked accurately.

Thursday afternoon, Robert Brentwood left his establishment and headed for the racetrack as he always did on Thursdays for as long as he can remember. Today would turn out differently from what he expected.

Antoine Bianco sat in his father's GMC, then followed Brentwood to the racetrack.

The Enforcer parked the GMC on the passenger side of the Cadillac. He punched a hole in the front and the back tires on the passenger side, causing the air to leak out.

Then Antoine moved the GMC to another parking space two cars away from the Cadillac and waited for Brentwood to return.

Hours later, Brentwood returned to his Cadillac. As he open the door on the driver's side, a lone figure wearing a grey hoodie walked up behind me and fired two shots into the back of Brentwood's head. The bookie was dead before the body hit the ground.

The Enforcer would eliminate the two men who beat his father to death. He found that killing came easy. Bianco decided to make a career out of contract killing.

Months after he took revenge for his father, he committed his mother (Maria Bianco) to a nursing home. She would get the care he couldn't provide for her on his own, and he could afford the payments to give his mother the best care.

Here he was on the Island of The Dominican Republic, thinking about going to a restaurant and socializing, something he couldn't ever remember doing.

Breaking his protocol, Antoine decides to go to the casino, have a meal, and play a few hands of poker. He would alter his appearance with a mustache, sideburns, and glasses.

Disguising came easily for The Enforcer. He has done this during his career. That's one thing that makes him so clever and dangerous.

At sixteen thirty, Drago stepped off the American Airlines flight. He picked up the reserved rental Range Rover and drove to the Hilton La Romana, where he checked in.

"Mr. Rick, this came in a few hours ago," the clerk behind the counter said, handing Drago a sealed envelope.

In his suite, Drago took off the white blazer and straw hat. He tossed both pieces of garment onto the bed and sat down.

Drago open the brown envelope and read the coded contents. The message informed him that The Enforcer was on the Island of The Dominican Republic.

As to his exact whereabouts, he would know as soon as they have his location.

It was still early in the afternoon. Rick called McCall, hoping to catch the Big Bossman before he left the office.

Dan McCall was reading the latest report on the fight between the Irish and the Russians in the Cayman Islands when the phone on his desk jangled, startling the big man.

McCall snatched it to his ear. "Yes," he said.

"Rick here. Any word on Antoine?"

"No."

"What about the battle in the Caymans?"

"The Russians were all wiped out by the Irish hit team."

"That's it then."

"No, it isn't. There was a drive-by shooting and a bombing in New Mexico and Arizona. The damn thing has spilled over on American soil."

"I'm not surprised. I will call my dad to see if he's alright."

"I know where your dad lives. It was not near to his place."

"I'll still call him. We haven't spoken for a while."

'We are waiting for confirmation on Russians living or vacationing on the Island of The Dominican Republic."

"Do you believe Antoine is here to carry out a hit?"

"Guys like The Enforcer do not take vacations as ordinary people do."

McCall's secretary knocked on the office door and entered. She then handed him a printout, which he read.

"They call for a sit-down," McCall said.

"The Irish and the Russians?"

"No. Only the Irish. All the bosses from Arizona and New Mexico will be there. The family needs to regroup and put an end to this conflict."

"When and where?"

"The meeting is scheduled for somewhere in the Caribbean."

"Do you think they will meet here?"

"Yes. I believe The Enforcer to be sure the place was safe."

"I see."

"Have you checked in with the Embassy?"

"I planned to go there today."

"Our man there is Len Darwin. He is young, smart, and good at his job. I've received nothing but praise about the young man. He may have information that can help you."

"I will see him."

"Remember. Len is not a field agent. He is a desk jockey sitting in front of a computer."

"Understand."

"You can't allow Antoine to slip away again."

"Will do my best," Drago assured McCall.

At nine am, Rick Drago went through the gates at Av: Republica de Colombia #57. Santo Domingo, Dominican Republic, and enters the American Embassy.

*Dominican Republic*

After showing his credentials. Drago met with Len Darwin.

"Good day, Mr. Drago," Len Darwin said with an outstretched hand.

Drago shook the young man's hand and noted how soft they were. McCall was right when he said Darwin was not a field agent.

"Hello," Drago replied.

"Follow me, please!" Darwin said, then turned and headed up the stairs to his office on the second landing.

"Please take a seat!" Len said, gesturing to a pair of chairs at the front of his desk.

At another much longer desk that took up the entire north side of the office sits three laptops and a desktop connected to a large screen.

The screen was displaying an area of the Island. The Province of La Altagracia is one of the most eastern places on the Island.

"We received information last night that may help you," Darwin said as he walked to the area displayed on the monitor.

Drago watched as Darwin continued to explain about the section of the map that he had circled.

"This is a highly established neighborhood. We believed the asset hiding out in Bavaro."

The news delighted Drago.

"Also, a few heads of the Irish families are due to arrive on the island tomorrow."

"Any word about where they will stay?"

"We believed Bavaro is where they will stay."

"They sent the Enforcer to be sure the place was safe for the meet."

"If you're right, the Irishmen should feel safe enough. I've got the names of the members who will attend the meeting right here," Darwin said, handing Drago a piece of paper.

Drago read the names and handed the paper back to Darwin.

"Do you have an address in Bavaro?" Drago asked.

"We know the location of the villa. The houses in that area don't have any identifying numbers."

"I see."

"We know the exact location of the villa. Here is the printout of it and the direction to get there," Darwin said, handing a piece of paper to Drago.

Drago examined the printout, then folded the paper and put it into one of his pockets.

"I am sorry. I couldn't be of more help."

"You did enough, much more than I had expected," Drago said.

"Good luck," Darwin said, shaking Drago's

hand.
    "Goodbye."

**Chapter Eleven**

After meeting with Darwin, Drago returned to his hotel and changed his clothes. His choice of clothing was now short khaki pants with cargo pockets on both legs, with an ocean green open-neck lapel shirt.

Drago put his gun in one of the pants' pockets and the other pocket. He put the silencer on and left the room.

Drago had no problem finding the house from the instructions given to him by Darwin. No vehicle was in the driveway at the house.

Drago drove by with the steady flow of traffic. On the other side of the road, across from the house, vehicles were parked.

Rick continued to drive about half a mile from the house. He pulled off the main road and waited until the road was clear, then turned and headed back.

Drago found a vacant area close to the house, big enough for the Range Rover. He parked the vehicle and waited, hoping to see the person staying there.

About an hour later, just before sunset, a vehicle pulled into the driveway leading to the house and stopped. A man fitting the description of Antoine Bianco got out and entered the building.

Drago waited until the sun descended into the water. As the darkness covered the area, he attached the silencer to the gun, tucked the weapon into the small of his back under the shirt, and got out of the vehicle.

Looking around and seeing that the area was clear, Drago crossed the road and went to the back of the house. As luck would have it, Drago got his break when he heard the shower running, and the silhouette of a man could be seen through the sliding shower door.

Drago fired, and the bullet entered Bianco's chest. The Enforcer slumped against the wall and slowly slid into the bathtub. Rick Drago then opened the shower door and secured the kill with a bullet in the center of Bianco's forehead.

After a quick search of the house, Drago found a cell phone and nothing else. However, the phone was locked and needed a passcode to open. Drago pocketed the phone and left the house.

Back in his rental, Drago called McCall on his private line.

"Yes. Rick," McCall said, seeing Drago's name on the screen.

"The package. Was delivered."

"Any other news?"

"I found an unbreakable mouthpiece."

"Darwin can help you with that. I will let him know that you will be coming to see him."

"Okay."

"Where are you now?"

"I am sitting behind the wheel, ready to drive away."

"Great job, Rick."

"My pleasure."

"Killing is a hard business. After a while, you start to lose some of your sharpness, and the body gets tired. That's what happened to Bianco."

"Perhaps. Maybe Bianco thought no one was looking for him on the Island."

"If the mouthpiece is a dead end. What are your plans?"

"I'll go to Arizona and see my dad, then to London."

"Okay. I'll be in touch if anything should turn up that needs your specialty."

The phones went dead as each man hung up. Drago then headed to visit his dad in Arizona.

Two days after Drago had left the Island of the Dominican Republic. Teddy Brennan, his brother Patrick Brennan, Rory Campbell, and Jackie Doyle. The four bosses of the Irish Family from Arizona and New Mexico flew into the Island on Teddy Brennan's private jet.

The moment the jet pulled up on the tarmac,

a stretched limo with dark tinted windows and a black Cadillac SUV with Four men inside was there to meet the men.

The men bolted off the jet into the limo. The driver was one of Teddy Brennan's men.

The four gunners in the SUV were the personal bodyguards of the bosses.

"Brendan, head to the town of Bavaro!" Teddy directed. "I'll tell you where to go."

"Okay, boss," replied Brendan. "The lawyer, Manuel Acosta, was trying to reach you."

"Did he leave a message?"

"No. All the Barrister said was. He needed to talk to you."

"Get him on the phone!" ordered Teddy. "Better yet. I'll call him."

The Lawyer informed Brennan about the killing of Antoine and what had to be done to keep the police from investigating the cause of death.

Manuel Acosta assured Brennan that the house was clean and safe for the group to stay. He had employed a couple of security guards to provide security for their safety.

They made arrangements that only the four bosses knew the place and time of the sit-down, thus reducing the possibility of a leak.

The two vehicles wheeled out from the airstrip and into the busy roadway.

For the first time since his cousin James Murphy got killed in Jamaica, Teddy felt much of the pressure lifted from his shoulders.

Brennan knew how much of a strain it could be, living in the shadows, under scrutiny from the law and opponents of the business he was dealing in. His nerves could handle only so much tension with the Russians.

When Brennan was a young man, he could handle the stress and solve problems quickly. Brennan had moved up through the ranks quickly because of the swift and no-nonsense way he got things done, but that was a long time ago when he'd been in his prime.

Brennan had decided that this trip to the Caribbean would do him some good. He would be sure to get plenty of rest at every opportunity.

Many things depended on Brennan being sharp, not only on the business side of the family, but also on the members who provided his security. He owes them to stay on top of the family business and be ready for anything. Brennan, not knowing where the Russians would strike next. And now, someone has taken out the elusive Antoine Bianco. Brennan hated the jittery feeling he was having in the pit of his stomach.

There was nothing Brennan could do at the moment, not knowing if a sniper would be waiting for him around the next corner or a load of hitmen to take out the family here on the Island.

Brennan and the other members of the Irish family were sure that the Russians did not know about the cottage on the Island of the Dominican Republic. But someone knew that Antoine Bianco (The Enforcer) was staying at the house and was successful in killing him.

As an added precaution, Acosta had hired off-duty police officers to provide security at the cottage to be sure it was safe when the Brennan arrived with the family.

The security guards weren't needed at the house any longer. The family members had brought their bodyguards along for the trip.

Situations like the present were why the family had purchased the cottage on the Island of the Dominican Republic. A place that provides solace, as well as to unwind in the beautiful atmosphere.

After settling in the villa, Brennan removed a small panel from the side of the power outlet breaker box and checked the tape recording captured from the mini-camera hidden in the ceiling above the fan.

Rick Drago had just set down his one piece of luggage in his room at his father's house when his cell phone buzzed.

"Not good timing, Rick," Dan said. "I just received word that something is in the wind coming out of Dominica." Dan paused, waiting for a response from Drago, which never came. "Word is. The Irish have issued a contract for you. Somehow, they found out you were the one that entered the house in Dominica and shot Antoine," Dan explained.

"How reliable is the info?" Drago asked.

"It came from our man down there, Len Darwin. Darwin got the intel from his contact in Interpol. appeared that Interpol bugged the house and picked up a message sent out to all the branches of the Irish family to issue the contract for your head."

"Okay."

"How do you want to handle this?"

Normally, Drago preferred to ply his trade solo or with his sometimes reliable partner Joanne. He and Joanne protect each other's back, trusting each other with their lives, and not to worry about a third person.

"Do you mind working with a few agents, as this is not a single asset you're up against? No one knows how many hitmen will be after your head. Joanne is not available at the moment."

"I was about to ask for her."

"Two excellent agents will assist you. They'll be waiting for you when you get here.

Agent Robinson graduated with top honors in long-range shooting. Harris's specialty is hand-hand, combat, and knife handling expert."

"I'll be there in the morning," Drago said.

"Fine. I made it clear they're to do whatever you say. See you tomorrow."

"Any other news?" Rick asked.

"Word out of New Mexico. An under-boss of the Irish family was gunned down as he went outside to collect the morning paper."

"Not smart."

"Who?"

"The Irish. The Russians are picking them off one by one, and now they want to take on the agency, by putting a contract on me? Not smart at all."

"Get some rest!" Dan said and hung up.

At seven o'clock, Drago got dressed in a v-neck T-shirt, khaki jacket, and pants, then headed to the airport for his flight to New York.

In New York, Drago entered Dan McCall's office. Two men sat in front of the desk.

"Have a seat!" Dan McCall said.

Drago sat down on the only available chair in the office. He then looked at the two men.

"I am Agent Robinson," said the man with the crew-cut hairstyle.

"And I am Agent Harris," the other man said, looking at the big Agent Code named the

Fixer. Questions seemed to lurk in his mind, but he dared not ask any, not knowing what the outcome would be, from his boss or the big man who just entered the room.

"Give us a moment," Dan said to Harris and Robinson. "You should go, and prepare the items you'll need to take!"

The two agents left the office and went to the weapons department.

"Was Robinson with the Agency long? I think I saw him before," Drago said to Dan.

"You saw his brother in Barbados a couple of years ago."

"Twins?"

"Yes. Both joined the Agency after the second tour of Afghanistan ended."

"What's the latest intel?" Drago asked.

"Here is what we know so far. The order came out of New Mexico, and it's an in-house contract."

"Fine."

"How do you want to handle it?"

"I'll start where the order originated."

"The Jet is fuel-up, and ready whenever you are."

"Anyone in New Mexico reliable?"

"Yes. Richard Barela. Richard owns and runs a jewelry store. Here is the address," Dan said, handing Drago a piece of paper, which the

Fixer memories then tore into pieces.

"Does he expect me?"

"No. We don't need a leak in this operation. Barela has provided us with information, from time to time, but people like him give out information to whoever is paying the most. He's a freelancer."

"Okay. Understood."

The sit down in Dominica lasted two days. It ended shortly after the men viewed the footage captured by the tiny hidden camera.

## Chapter Twelve

Teddy Brennan, "Big Ted" to those who knew him, sat in the back of his limo with three bodyguards. He returned home to New Mexico after returning from The Republic Of Dominica.

Two bodyguards sat in the front seat, and one sat beside him in the back seat.

Big Ted always had a weakness for red wine, and Onion flavored Pringles. Teddy managed to stay in good shape thanks to the young brunette who put him through a rigorous weekly workout.

A few years back, Teddy Brennan lost his wife to cancer. He vows never to get married again. Teddy loved being in the company of females. It didn't matter if they were black or white, as long as they had a nice body and a beautiful face.

Brennan would entertain scores of pretty women during the week. Many of his associates envied him and they also wondered how a man at that age could handle so many women.

Today was no exception. He was on his way to a lunch date with a gorgeous blonde whom he met a few days before heading to the sit-down in Dominica.

Teddy Brennan changed his style of living after losing his wife to cancer. "Life is too short to worry about petty things. I hope you guys are investing your money for the future," he'd say to his bodyguards.

"Say Boss," the driver remarked. "What time is your expecting you?"

"Whenever I get there. Why do you ask?"

"Looks like a backup of traffic up ahead."

Minutes ago, they had turned onto Central Avenue and came smack into bumper-to-bumper vehicles. The traffic crawled until they passed a jack-knife truck that caused the traffic to use one lane.

A person wearing a white helmet approached the back door of the Limo and quickly snapped a tiny transmitter under the top of the wheel well.

"Just great," Brennan said. "Hope it's not one of ours."

"I don't think so, boss," the driver replied.

Brennan looked at his watch.

"I am running late," he growled.

"Not to worry, Boss. I'll have you there in no time."

Rick Drago and his two associates sat in a grey Range Rover a short distance from the truck. Robinson sat behind the wheel. He then started the engine and waited until the limo-carrying Brennan passed. He then followed, keeping two vehicles between the limo and the Ranger.

Twenty minutes later, the limo turned into the parking lot of a restaurant. The driver of the limo and another of the bodyguards got out and entered the building. The men came out through a side door of the restaurant, stood by the door, and waited until Brennan got out of the car and went through the open door.

Despite the delay caused by the jack-knifed truck, the driver got his boss to the restaurant at the pre-arranged time, which was 3 pm, one hour before the official opening time, 4. pm.

Two of the bodyguards waited outside by the side door, the other took a seat at the bar.

Brennan was early for his date. As he waited, sipping on a glass of red wine, a tall black man entered.

Robinson and Harris approached the

bodyguards. The attack happened so fast that the two guards didn't have time to react.

Drago entered through the front door. His right hand was in the pocket of the khaki jacket and holding the 38.-Special with the silencer attached. From the pocket, Drago shot the bodyguard sitting at the bar, then shoved the gun into Brennan's ribs.

"Up. Let's go!" Drago ordered.

Only the manager and the chef were on duty, as the restaurant wasn't to open until the next hour. The two men turned their heads when Drago shoved Brennan out of the dining area and through the side door.

Harris sat at the wheel of Brennan's limo. Drago pushed the Irish boss into the back seat with Robinson. Then Harris pulled out of the parking area.

"Pulled the contract you ordered on the agent!" Drago ordered.

"I can't," Brennan replied.

Robinson smacked Brennan across the face with the muzzle of his gun.

"Yes, you can," Robinson said.

"Do It now!"

Harris turned the limousine into the public underground parking area of the central mall.

Brennan, realizing he had no way of getting away from his captures, made the call to pull the contract.

"Now. You will give me the names and where to find the hitmen on the list to carry out the hit, plus your underbosses," Drago said as he handed Brennan a piece of paper and a pen.

The Irish boss did as he was told, then gave the paper with the names and places to Drago, who then punched the information into his phone and sent it to Dan McCall.

From the back seat of the limo, they took Brennan and put him into the trunk.

"I hope you made peace with your maker before you left your home today," Harris said as he shot Brennan on his forehead and closed the trunk.

Patrick Brennan was the next boss under his Brother Teddy.

Unlike his brother "Big Ted," he lived modestly. Never married, but lived with the same female partner for many years. Patrick has one son from a previous relationship. And shares joint custody with the boy's mother.

His two-story house was not extravagant by any standard. The only standout different from his neighbors was the high walls around the structure and the mounted cameras.

The lawn and garden were like any other house in the neighborhood.

This gated neighborhood of Las Campanas

would cause an entry problem for most, but for the AWB agents, it may not be.

The sun was setting when Drago and his team reached the upscale community.

Harris's cell phone buzzed. "Yes. I understand. I will pass it on," he said.

"What's up?" Robinson asked.

"That was Mark Glasser. The address of Patrick Brennan is in a gated neighborhood."

"We already know that. What else did he say about the other names I sent him?" Drago asked.

"He was trying to contact you. He said something is wrong with your cell."

Drago checked his phone and noticed that it had turned off.

"What now?" Robinson asked.

"We wait," Drago said.

Rick Drago's cell phone chirped. He listened in between "Uh huh, got it", the person on the other end did most of the talking.

"That was Dan. The feds are looking into the shooting at the restaurant in Albuquerque," Drago said after he turned off his cell.

"That didn't take long," Harris stated. "I also notice you never said sir or boss during the conversation."

"Yes. Why is that?" Robinson quizzed.

The Fixer had no ready answer to their question.

"It seemed that Patrick Brennan likes to play the game of poker and goes to the casino weekly to have a game."

"Let me see how smart I am," Robinson said. "Tonight is his visit to the casino."

"Yes. We also have the plates of his limo."

Drago showed the number on the plate to Harris and Robinson, as it appeared on the cell phone screen.

The Fixer knew he had to hasten and get to Patrick Brennan before he received word of his brother's demise. Knowing it would become much harder to get to him, as the protection would be increased dramatically.

Minutes before the restaurant in Albuquerque opened to the public for business, the manager called the local police headquarters and reported that a shooting had taken place and three men were shot and killed.

Agents of the local F.B.I. were called in after the three dead men were identified as members of the mob.

The Feds put an all-points bulletin for Teddy Brennan's limo after they realized that the three dead men were his bodyguards.

Someone had taken the limo and the Irish boss. The description the Feds received from the restaurant manager and the chef was sketchy.

According to the manager, it was one man

who came in through the front door, shot the bodyguard sitting at the bar, then took Teddy Brennan at gunpoint and left.

The chef gave a completely different version of the events. He insisted they were two men. Brennan got into the back of the car at gunpoint, and another person was sitting at the wheel and drove away, heading south towards the freeway.

Soon after the call from McCall ended, the gates opened and the limo carrying Patrick Brennan exited, followed by a dark-colored Cadillac SUV with tinted windows.

"Time for some serious work," Harris said, starting the Cadillac SUV, similar to the one following Patrick Brennan's limo, and pulled out. He kept three car lengths behind the mob convoy. When they slowed, Harris did the same. When they sped up, he sped up.

"What were we doing before?" Robinson asked.

"Those guys with Teddy were standing targets. I have a feeling it's going to be a lot tougher with this bunch," Harris responded.

"Don't lose the asset," Drago commanded.

"When do we take them?" Robinson asked.

"We wait and see where they are going. If Patrick goes to the casino, he will use the valet parking service," the Fixer said.

"The floors are all connected in the

underground parking at the casinos," Robinson said.

"You know what to do," the Fixer remarked.

"Where will you be?"

"I'll be in the casino, taking in a hand of poker," Drago replied.

"Mind if I tag along? You may need an extra pair of eyes," Robinson suggested.

"Harris may need your help more than I."

"You guys go ahead. I'll be alright," Harris said upon hearing the remark that Drago made to Robinson.

Drago had a decision to make. Should they engage with these guys at the casino or wait until they leave? The Fixer decides after they leave the casino.

A place at a nearby poker table was available. Drago sat down and started to play. Robinson chose a slot machine in full view of Drago.

One hour later, Patrick Brennan got up from the poker table immediately. Two men sitting at the same table as Drago got up and joined Brenn as he headed for the door.

The mob boss ducked into his limousine. Two men got into the back with Patrick, and one into the front seat with the driver.

Five men into the Cadillac SUV. The convoy wheeled from the casino driveway and left, heading in a different direction from the route they took from his home. "Where the hell can they be going?" Harris wondered.

"Does Patrick own another house?" Robinson asked.

"Many of the mafia bosses have more place to hideout. They like to have a p sanctuary away from prying eyes," Drago said.

The outskirts of the town faded as the convoy moved along the freeway. The str along the side of the highway was far from each other.

Hell In Paradise

The moon was full and shining brightly. Traffic got lighter the further away from the town they drove.

Harris looked into the rear-view mirror. "I think we've picked up a tail," he said.

Drago checked the traffic behind them. He saw the two headlights fast approaching them. "Maybe you are right."

"What now?" Robinson asked.

"Let's be sure it's us they are trying to catch up to," Drago stated.

Harris slowed the SUV to let the approaching vehicle pass. Shots rang out when the sedan came abreast with the SUV.

Quick action by Harris stepping on the brakes allowed the car to go in front. Robinson returned fire, breaking the back window, then hitting and blowing out the left back tire.

The sedan skidded sideways, then flipped over on its side.

"Move it!" the Fixer commanded.

Harris increased the speed. Within minutes, he had closed the distance and was at the side of the SUV that carried the gunners. The vehicle had slowed, allowing the limousine to get a distance ahead.

Bumper to bumper along the freeway, trying to push each other off the road. Then, the Fixer rolled the back window down. He got LCR.38 Special, and the Fixer fired. The bullet entered at the base of the left ear, exiting through the right side of the jaw.

The SUV broke through the guardrail, then rolled down into the ravine and broke into flames.

Drago looked back to see the smoke from where the vehicle went through the guardrail.

"Guess we won't see them again," Robinson said.

"I think not," Harris agreed. "One more to go."

## Chapter Thirteen

The brake lights from the limousine appeared ahead. "I believe they are about to turn off the freeway," Harris suggested.

"Do you think Patrick made a call for more support?" Robinson asked.

"If I was him. Sure," Harris said.

The limousine turned off the freeway and onto an unpaved road. A cloud of white dust from the tires as the car hurried along on the road.

The dust made the turnoff easy to find. A large sign informed everyone that it was a private road and that no one was permitted to enter without an invitation. Harris followed the trail of white dust. The road curved to the right, close to a small ravine, then straight again.

A grey stone structure appeared up ahead,. Patrick Brennan's limousine was across the road, blocking any approaching vehicles.

"I will go after Patrick. The two of you will deal with the gunners and any others who try to rescue the boss," the Fixer said.

Drago double-checked his ammo, then took two more clips from the care package and got out of the SUV when Harris brought it to a stop. He moved behind the SUV when the hail of bullets erupted as the gunners used the limo as a shield.

Robinson and Harris slid out of the car and returned fire. Drago was crouched and moved swiftly along the edge of the road, heading for the house. Robinson crawled to the back of the SUV and took a rifle with a night scope and silencer attached.

Using the opened back door of the SUV, Robinson took out two of the gunners. The other man made a run for it, heading towards the house. The man was face to face with Drago as they reached the door together.

Drago, without hesitation, fired a kill shot. The bullet hit the gunner just below the temple. The man was dead before his body hit the ground.

It was once a sprawling, beautifully crafted building made from limestone. Scaffolding on the side of the structure suggests that work had recently begun refurbishing the house. Vines that once cluttered around the windows were now lying on the ground. A huge waste container was up against the corner of the house, filled with rubbish.

The Fixer took a quick look around for any movement. Satisfied that no one else was there, he reached for the handle.

Drago tugged on the handle, then slowly opened the door. With his back against the wall, he swiftly moved further into the house. There was a door on the right side of the hallway slightly ajar. The Fixer used the silencer and pushed the door open wider. He looked inside. The room was empty. There was no sign of the Irish Skipper.

Going further into the house, Drago entered

what looked like the living room. A large screen TV hung on the left wall. Pieces of furniture covered with plastic. At the dining table, sitting with a bottle of wine and two glasses, was Patrick Brennan.

"I have been expecting you," Brennan said. The Fixer signaled with his gun for Brennan to stand up. He then patted the man down, searching him for any weapons, finding none.

"Sit!" Drago commanded.

"So. You are the one who is creating havoc between us and the Russians."

"I got involved because of the hitman you had hired."

"You are talking about Antoine Bianco?"
"Yes. I took him out, but someone in your organization put a contract on me."

"That was my brother. He realized it was a mistake to get the agency involved, bringing more heat on us with the conflict we have going with the Russians."

Hell In Paradise

"Why didn't he cancel the contract?"

"He did."

"Yes, he did. That was after I caught up to him in Albuquerque."

"Where is my brother now?"

"You can say hello when you meet him."
"Where are we going?"

"He is already there waiting for you."

Before Patrick could say another word, the Fixer put a bullet in the center of his forehead, then he left the house.

Robinson and Harris watched Drago come out of the house and rejoin them.

"Let's get out of here," Drago said.

"Did you find Patrick?" Harris asked.

"Yes. I send him to be with his brother," the Fixer replied.

"What's next?" Robinson enquired.

Two headlights and a cloud of dust from an approaching vehicle caught the eyes of the Agents. "We have company," Harris said.

"Yes. They are coming fast," Robinson stated. "Brennan got a message out for more help," Harris suggested.

"Let's take them out quickly and be on our way!" Drago said.

Robinson took his position to the left side of Drago. Harris took the right side. Drago got into a crouch position, as a bullet shattered the windshield and found its mark, hitting the driver in his neck. The man threw his hands to his neck and screamed.

A man sitting next to him lunged at the steering wheel and tried to bring the car under control, to no avail.

The vehicle traveling over forty miles per

hour, slanted to the right side, hit tiny trees and went airborne. The tires were spinning when it plowed into a thicket of thick bushes.

Then, the agents lost sight of the car as it went into the bushy area. A loud sound indicated that the vehicle had come to a stop.

Drago leaped over many broken bushes and small trees, followed by Robinson and Harris. The vehicle was lying on its side, the front end was lodged against a mound of mud and stone.

The body of the driver was slumped forward on the steering wheel. The airbag had deployed and the use of the seatbelt saved him from going through the windshield.

The engine stopped, steam spewed from the broken radiator, and the smell of gas coming from the ruptured gas line.

A gunner sitting in the front wasn't as lucky. It looks like he didn't have his seatbelt connected, and went through the windshield after the impact of the vehicle and the embankment. He was lying in front of the car, bleeding from a puncture in his chest. Cautiously Drago stepped closer, then he knelt beside the man and felt for a pulse. The man was dead.

The back door on the driver's side flew open as Robinson and Harris walked to the back of the vehicle.

A gunner pushed up his head, blood from a

cut above the eyebrow flowing into the eye, blurring his vision. The man began spitting blood and rubbing his eyes, trying to clear his vision.

The gunner cleared his vision in time to see the two agents approaching. "Bastards!" the man shouted, raising a gun. It would've been smarter. On his part, to keep the weapon hidden.

Harris threw a knife. The blade found its mark, piercing into the forearm of the gunner. The gun fell from his hand over the side of the vehicle.

Robinson and Harris assist the man out of the vehicle. Looking inside, they saw that the other gunner jammed between the front and back seats. And he was holding an Uzi in his right hand. Holes in the passenger seat in the front suggest that the gun fired bullets into the seat after the gunner got pinned.

Drago joined Robinson and Harris as they pulled the man from the car.

"There's another man in there, pinned behind the passenger seat," Harris stated.

"Alive or dead?" Drago asked.

"We're not sure," Robinson replied. "Let's make sure," Drago urged.

Robinson and Harris yanked the door open after pulling the gunner through the broken window and putting him on the ground.

Then Robinson reached in and removed the Uzi from the hand of the injured man. He pulled the man by the shoulder and dislodged him from against the seat.

"No pulse. This guy is dead," Robinson said. "Let's find out what this guy knows!" Drago suggested.

The gunner lay on the stomach with his head turned to the right side. The blood continued coming through his mouth. Drago squatted over him and felt for a pulse. "He's no longer with us," he said.

Unable to get any information from anyone. Drago, Robinson, and Harris got into the SUV and drove away from the scene.

Agent Harris sat behind the wheel, Drago riding shotgun, and Robinson sat in the back.

They had proceeded a short distance when Drago's cell phone beeped. The Fixer answered. He listened to the person on the other end without interrupting. His only word was "understood."

"You are to return to New York at once," the Fixer said.

"And you? What about you?" Robinson asked. "I have some other important matters to attend."

"Will we ever see you again?"

"In our business, you never can predict

what's going to happen," Drago said.

"It was a pleasure working with you," Harris said.

"That goes for me," Robinson exclaimed.

"The feeling is mutual,"

"Where should I take you?" Harris asked.

"The airport."

"So. The contract on you, was it canceled?" Robinson asked.

"I am unsure if word has reached all the people involved in issuing the order to their members."

Rory Hayes, a top lieutenant to Jackie Doyle in Arizona, had an unscheduled meeting with his boss.

"I need to know exactly how many of our people we have lost in the past few days," Jackie Doyle said impatiently, tapping his left foot on the floor, something he always does when he gets angry.

"Teddy and Patrick Brennan have lost members of their crew."

"You are supposed to know this, give me a number!" Doyle scowled.

"I think nine or ten soldiers, along with the Brennans."

"Someone has to go to New Mexico and take control until we elect a new king," Doyle said, picking up his cell phone and making a call.

Rory Hayes waited until his boss ended his call.

"Teddy Brennan's clan chief is coming from Jamaica to take over in New Mexico. There's no word on Teddy, only Patrick. As of last night, they found his body in a ranch house he recently bought."

"We must believe that Teddy is dead," Rory stated.

"Teddy brought that on himself when he took on the feds, knowing we had the Russians to deal with."

"He pulled the contract," Rory said.

"Yes. And no one has seen Teddy after he did." Doyle said. "The Feds probably have him on ice."

"Does this give you more power within the family?" Rory asked.

"Now that Danny Campbell is out of Jamaica. He will act as the Skipper in New Mexico until we appoint a new Skipper. So, someone has to go to Jamaica and take his position."

"Are you sending me down there?"

"It would be a great opportunity for you to move up. You will be in charge of the crew we have down there."

Rory looked at his boss with a broad smile.

"I appreciate the offer."

"So. You accept?"

"Of course. I do," Rory Hayes replied. "What about Campbell? Doesn't he have someone in mind?"

"No. You were the chosen one." "Great. When will I leave?"

"As soon as you are ready."

"Can I take the family?"

"First, you go. Check the place out and see if it will be good for your family to move there. Only you can make that decision."

"I will do as you suggested."

### *Jamaica*

Noel Charles and his posse, along with the remaining members of the Irish crew, had maintained control of the drugs coming in and going out through the Port of Ocho Rios in Jamaica.

The Russians lost many of their soldiers during the shoot-out they had a Jamaican/Irish mob in the Cayman Islands.

The Irish also lost members of their crew, but the toll was not as high as the Russians.

Noel Charles had recruited more people to become members of his posse, replacing the ones who died in the Cayman Islands.

Business was good again. There were no more interruptions in the shipments. Everything went smoothly. The Irish and Jamaicans were making money.

They added three large containers to the side of the warehouse, creating more storage room for Noel Charles. The business had expanded to importing and distributing artifacts and shipping automobiles to parts of Asia and Africa.

Noel Charles expanded his network to the Republic of Haiti and the Dominican Republic.

The two Republic countries are a couple of hundred miles east of Jamaica, making it the perfect place for Noel Charles to set up shop for his distributing business.

Rory Hayes has always promised himself if he ever got a crew, they would become the best in the family. Each man would have to do his duty or be dismissed from the team. Hayes hoped he could fill the shoes of Danny Campbell, or even do a better job. Part of his responsibility was the protection of Daniel O'Brien, who had taken over the operation of the Hotel Grand Casino, after the demise of his cousin James Murphy.

The Irish mob began beefing up the protection for all the bosses after the death of James Murphy. The Irish family realized that having two bodyguards was not good enough to protect the bosses in the family.

That was proven when Patrick Brennan tried to get away from what they thought was a Russian hit team following him when he left the casino. Instead of going to his home in the gated community, Patrick made it to what he believed would be his safe house. His team of bodyguards could not save him from his pursuers. As a result, Patrick was executed sitting at the dining table.

Because the Irish mob lost the Brennan brothers in such a timely manner. They recruited new people to replace the soldier's lives in the past few weeks. The Russian mob did the same as the Irish, preparing for the next battle.

The Russians brought in Igor Sokolov, a retired lieutenant from the Spetsnaz, the most elite unit in the Russian army. With Sokolov in charge, the Russians believe they have a good chance of destroying the Irish mob.

The retired lieutenant had always prided himself on running a tight outfit. His men were the best of the best. They received the best equipment, food, and training. It will be a challenge training civilians to become a fighting unit.

The Russians didn't want to lose any more of their mob members. The idea was for Sokolov to recruit and train the people, then accompany the team to help secure control over the Irish mob and wipe them out.

Fedorov had survived the fighting in the Cayman Islands. His underboss wasn't so lucky. Fedorov brought in his eldest son, Anton Fedorov Jr to be his underboss. With his military background, he should feel at home giving orders to other members.

Two Irish skippers, Rory Campbell and Jackie Doyle, decided that Danny Campbell, although he was never a Clan Chief. Campbell, being a cousin to the Brennan's, should take control in New Mexico until a new Skipper was appointed.

Jackie Doyle called a meeting to look at prospective candidates to replace the two deceased Skippers.

The meeting would be at Jackie Doyle's hide-away cottage outside Florence in Fiesole.

*New Mexico*

Skippers and clan chiefs from around the country showed up and voted for the candidates who should fill the vacancies.

Doyle had given Campbell a tour of the shortly after he arrived. Jackie had guards posted at strategic points around the cottage. He wanted everyone to feel safe while staying at the house.

"This is your safe place?" Campbell asked. "I think it can serve as such."

"How many candidates are you expecting?" "We have Danny Campbell. I know he is a cousin of Ted Brennan. But, is he a relative of yours?"

"No. I checked him out a long time ago. The answer is he's not a family member."

"Along with Danny, we have your second in command. Two more coming from Jersey and one from Frisco."

"That totals five to fill two positions." "Yes."

"What about your second in command?" Rory Campbell asked.

"No. I need him here with me. He will take my place when I step down."

Minutes later, a tall man standing over six feet and weighing about two hundred and thirty pounds walks into the room.

This was Jackie Doyle's Clan Chief, Aidan Collins, ex-football player and martial arts expert.

"Bring us a bottle of scotch, will you?" Jackie said.

The big man brought a bottle of single malt with two glasses and put them on the table.

"Do you know Rory Campbell?" Jackie asked Aidan.

"Only by reputation," Aidan replied. "Nice to meet you," with a large outstretched hand.

Rory took the hand. "The feeling is mutual." Each man poured a drink into a glass, glasses touched, then raised.

Both men took a sip of Scotch and then put their glasses on the table.

Kings and clan chiefs arrive at the cottage. They were ushered into the prepared room for the meeting and sat down at the vast table.

In front of each seat were plates, cutlery, glasses, and bottles of wine, both white and red.

Servers from the catering company stood nearby to take orders requiring beverages other than wine.

One such man was Brendan Bryne, nicknamed to his friends as B&B. Brendan was a big man, a former bodybuilder and Olympic wrestling champion. He stood six feet six inches and weighed about two hundred and fifty pounds, with massive arms and broad shoulders, with fists, when folded, would be the size of about nine and a half inches.

"Bring me a bottle of whiskey! He ordered." Brendan poured a glass of the beverage, then took a slurp of half before putting the glass back on the table.

"This is very distressing. Two of our Skippers lost in such a short time," Brendan said.

"Yes," the skipper from Jersey said. "What are we going to do about that?"

"Let's hear what Rory and Jackie say," Brendan advised.

"Agreed." another man said.

Rory Campbell and Jackie Doyle joined the other skippers. Looking around, Jackie saw some familiar faces. He moved around the table, exchanging pleasantries with those he knew and receiving introductions to the ones he didn't.

Rory Campbell did the same and began shaking hands among friends, using first names only. After the hellos and introductions, Jackie sat at the head of the table, and Campbell took the seat at the right of Jackie Doyle.

After selecting candidates to replace the two kings, a new king of kings had to be chosen to replace Teddy Brennan.

"We have to elect someone to replace Teddy as head of the family!" Brendan Bryne said.

The kings and clan chiefs got up from the table and entered another room.

"Jackie Doyle is the best person to be our King of kings," Rory Campbell said. "All those agreed, signify by saying, aye."

Brendan Bryne sniffed. "I think it would be obvious to everyone that Jackie should lead us."

"I agree," Campbell stated.

There were no objections to appointing Jackie Doyle, the king of all kings.

"We have much to do. I don't want to lose another king or a clan chief, or any soldier, for that matter," Doyle said. "Has anyone heard anything about the Russians?"

"The Russians must have heard about Teddy and Patrick," the newly appointed king of New Mexico said.

"Yes. I thought about that," Brendan said.

"We have to believe the Russians know about Ted and Pat."

"Do you think they are the ones that carried out the hit?" a clan chief asked.

"Not on Teddy. that a squad of specially trained men did within women's government," Doyle stated. "We know that from the description the manager and the chef at the restaurant gave to the investigating officers."

"So. you think the Feds are holding Ted?" Brendan asked.

"Until his body shows up, we must believe he's still alive," Doyle said.

"And Patrick? What about him? Do you believe the Russians had something to do with his death?" the clan chief from Los Angeles asked.

"I don't know for sure. They weren't any survivors," Doyle explained.

"We have to do something. Everyone has to do their part and try to find out what happened to Teddy. We owe it to the family."

"I will appoint some of my men to investigate. In the meantime, we have to keep our guard up. The Russians were on one side.

"The feds got involved after Teddy Brennan gave the order to put a contract on one of their agents," Oscar O'Brien, the king from Boston, said.

"Yes. That was not a good idea. What's done is done. We have to move on, and plan the future of this family," Doyle said.

"Agreed," Brendan said.

"That should do it for the time being," Jackie Doyle said. "Remember the slightest whisper about the Russians or Teddy Brennan? Treat it with most eagerness, and inform everyone."

Robinson and Harris boarded the plane to the New York office. Drago's phone buzzed.

"Yes. Boss," he said, answering the phone on the third buzz.

"Rick. You're needed in Haiti. As you know, we have a new ambassador there. His name is Douglas McArthur. He has a teenage daughter. It seems she's been missing for two days."

"Why doesn't he call the local police?"

"This is Haiti. Everyone on the island is corrupt, including some members of the law enforcement."

"The Ambassador is a friend of a friend. You know how it goes."

"Forty-eight hours? You know that after that time has passed, it becomes harder to find anyone. She could be on the way to the Far East or sold to a human trafficker."

"He's hoping that hasn't happened."

"You spoke to him?"

"Yes. I did."

"What you're not telling me, Dan? What happened to his daughter?"

"She's a substance misuse. He believes she found her way to a crack house."

"That's a dangerous place, more dangerous for Americans."

"He asks if you're available."

"And?"

"I told him I would see what I could do, but I wasn't making any promises."

"Do I know him?"

"No. I don't think so," Dan said. "His dad knows your dad. The two of them served together in the Marines. They remained friends."

"What's my status?" Drago asked.

"Diplomat. Under the name of Richard Gibson. Special liaison health inspector."

"When am I expected there?"

"As soon as possible. Time is of the essence." "I know."

"The jet will be ready in three hours. Everything that you need will be onboard."

## *Haiti*

Four hours later. Drago's private jet touched down on the tarmac in Port-au-Prince. The deputy ambassador was there to meet Drago as he got off the plane in a chauffeur-driven SUV.

"You must be Mr. Richard Gibson," the deputy said with an outstretched hand.

"And you are?"

"I am the Deputy Ambassador." Thomas Pickerman.

"What has been done about finding the young woman?"

"The Ambassador was trying to keep it low-key using our people from the office to find out what happened."

"Were they successful in getting any leads on the young woman"?

Thomas Pickerman handed a folder to Drago.

"You will find the information accumulated in the folder."

Rick Drago read the contents of the files in

the folder. "Cite Soleil. Where is that?" he asked.

"Cite Soleil is a shantytown on the outskirts of Port-au-Prince."

"I would like to talk to the person who got the information on Cite Soleil."

"He can be available to aid you if you need him."

"Just a few questions I have to ask him."

At the Embassy they introduce Dick Drago to the staff as Richard Gibson, a liaison specialist in health care.

Drago then met with Ambassador McArthur in his office.

"Do you have any instructions on how you want me to proceed with finding your daughter and getting her back safe and sound to you?"

"I leave that to you. This was hand delivered at the gate a few minutes before you arrived," the Ambassador said, handing Drago a brown envelope.

Sherwin A. Goodman

## Chapter Fourteen

Drago opened the envelope and read the note written badly in English. "We have your daughter. We will contact you again later."

"This changes everything," Drago stated.

"Yes. it does."

"Alright. Can I have a printout of the area where your daughter was last seen?"

"Richard will help you with that."

Drago got up from the table, shook hands with the Ambassador, and left the office.

Thomas Pickerman was waiting for Drago

when he left the Ambassador's office.

"Shall we go to my office? David Haggerty is waiting there," Pickerman said.

"David? Oh, the man with the information about Cite Soleil?"

"Yes. He can go with you and show you where the girl was last seen."

Drago left the Embassy with David, who sat behind the wheel of the S.U.V.

David drove along Boulevard Jean-Jacques Dessalines, heading for Cite Soleil.

Drago viewed the destruction of the colonial buildings along the stretch of the Grande Rue, as named by the residents.

They hand wrote the name on a piece of tin on every street corner that branches off the Grande Rue.

On electric polls display Blvd JJD. The Grande Rue was crowded with people, tap-tap, donkey carts, and bicycles, as the street served as the gateway to many villages.

"Here we are," David said, stopping the SUV in front of a large ruined structure.

David and Drago got out of the vehicle. David carried a camera strapped over his shoulder. The two men walked up the steps, carefully stepping over fallen concrete slabs.

Drago entered what looked like a makeshift home. Someone had secured many sheets of galvanized material to provide shelter from the elements. Rocks and pieces of metal made a fire pit for cooking. In one corner, sheets hung from the galvanized to the floor, giving the person privacy.

"Bonswa," David said in Haitian Creole.

He received no reply. David slipped the sheets aside and looked behind them. "There's no one here."

"Did you receive the information from the person staying here?"

"Yes."

"This person, man or woman?"

"A young man, he was in the company of a young girl. She could be his girlfriend."

"Did you pay him?"

"Yes. I gave him three US dollars. That's around four hundred Haitian Groude, a significant amount of money for these people."

"Let's find out if anyone else staying in this place has seen the girl."

Many squatters were living throughout the damaged building. They were syringes lying around on the ground. The filthy odor mixed with the smell of drugs gave a terrible stench from some chambers as the two agents went further through the building.

A woman approached the Agents. "What are you doing here?" she asked in broken English.

"We are looking for a young American girl. She was here days ago," Drago said.

"Have you seen her?" David asked. "Yes. The girl was high on drugs, then two men came and took her away," the woman replied. "Do you know where the men took her?" "I heard somewhere in the city."

"Port-au-Prince? They took her to Port-au-Prince?" Drago asked.

"Yes. That's what I heard."

"Do have the name of the place they took the girl? Was it a street, a house?" David asked.

"The only other thing. The men spoke Patois."

"Not Haitian?" David asked.

"Patois is a Jamaican dialect."

"I know," Drago replied.

"No. They were not Haitian. They had locks."

"Jamaicans?"

"The men that took her were Jamaicans," David stated.

David handed the woman a few Haitian Groude. The woman took the money, bowed, and backed away from the Agents.

"Nothing more to do here," Drago said. "Do you have any contacts in the city? You know, an informate/ snitch."

"Yes. I tried reaching him two days ago but

didn't," David said. "He's not a snitch as such. He is a cop. From time to time, he and I share information."

"Let's find him. You know where he lives?" Drago asked.

"Yeah, I do. He has an apartment in Petionville. But he has many female friends. I have to call to know where he is."

David got his cell phone and punched in a few numbers. He puts the phone on the speaker system so Drago can hear.

"Hello, David," the man on the other end said. "Hello, Paul."

"I was about to call you," Paul Guillaume stated.

"You have something for me?"

"Yes. Not on the phone. Where are you now?" "I'm on Grande Rue, close to Belair. We were Cite Soleil."

"Okay. Let's meet at the last place we saw each other."

"I'm on my way."

"See you in a few," Paul said, then turned off his phone.

Paul was waiting at the Papillon Enterprise shopping mall when David Haggerty and Drago arrived.

The three men found a vacant table and sat down.

"Paul. This is Richard Gibson. He is in charge of the investigation," David said, introducing Drago.

The two men shook hands. "Please to meet you," Paul said.

"Same here," Drago replied.

"What do you have for me?" David asked. "The information I got from one of my people on the street. A gang of Jamaicans was holding her."

"Where? Do you know where she's being held?" Drago asked.

"Somewhere in the commercial district close to the waterfront. I was told that the Jamaicans have a business vendor somewhere there."

"You are talking about Delmas?" David asked. "Delmas? Yes. That's a commercial area, and it's close to the canal," Paul confirmed.

"Where is Delmas?" Drago asked.

"It's an area east of the major city of Port-au-Prince," Paul answered.

Drago checked the time on his watch. The timepiece was showing seventeen hundred hours.

"Can we visit the area now? I would like to have a look at it," Drago said.

"The traffic will be heavy this time of the day," Paul informed Rick.

"He is right," David agreed.

"The longer it takes, it will become more difficult to find her," Drago said.

Rick Drago's cell phone buzzed. He answered and listened to the voice on the other end.

"Yes. Dan, I will go there right away." "We are called back to the embassy," Drago said to David.

"I will find out what I can and get back to you," Paul said as the three men parted company. "What gives?" David asked, getting behind the steering wheel.

Hell In Paradise

"Things have changed." "For the good or bad?"

"We'll find out at the Embassy."

Back at the American Embassy, the staff was busy on computers, punching in information and waiting for replies.

"They are waiting for you, sir," a red-haired young man said to Drago when he entered the Embassy.

Drago looked at him with a puzzled gaze.

"Follow me! Sir."

Drago followed the man up one flight of stairs. Reaching the first landing, they turned right, then walked along the corridor displaying portraits on both walls of former ambassadors to Haiti.

The young officer Knock. Then opened the door, stepped aside for Drago to enter the room, and then closed the door.

Ambassador McArthur and his deputy, Thomas Pickerman, sat at a table looking over stacks of papers.

"Come in!" McArthur said, looking up from the papers in front of him.

"We have a dilemma," Pickerman said.

"I see," Drago responded. "What gives?" "The people holding my daughter believe this embassy can influence the outcome of the proceedings about to take place against a pilot whose small plane crashed a few weeks ago carrying drugs and something valuable,"

"Who is the pilot?"

"His name is Rudy Auckerman," Pickerman said. "The Ambassador's daughter will be free when they release the pilot."

"Is he an American?"

"Yes. Rudy was a pilot during the war in Afghanistan," Pickerman said.

"Here's what we have on him," the ambassador said, handing a file to Drago.

The photo of a bald white male was attached to the folder, with the name Rudy Auckerman.

## Chapter Fifteen

Drago read the contents of the file. "Two tours in Afghanistan," he said out loud. "Honorable discharge."

"A clean military record," Pickerman said.

"What about family?"

"There's no mention of any family in his file," the deputy ambassador said.

"Okay. When does Rudy go before the court?" Drago asked.

"The trial was postponed twice. The new date is two days from now," Pickerman explained.

"Where is Rudy being held?" Drago asked.

"I know the place," the deputy said.

"I will leave the two of you. Other duties need my attention," Ambassador McArthur said as he got up from the table and left the room.

"Let's get David in here!" Drago suggested.

"You have a plan?"

"Yes. I do."

"May I ask what it is?"

"It is best that you or Ambassador McArthur don't know about it."

"I understand. Of course. That's why you are here."

"David. When he gets here, I need you to leave the room."

"Do you need any more information from me?"

"Leave everything you found out about Rudy Auckerman with me. I will return it to you."

The deputy ambassador left the room.

Minutes later, David Haggerty joined Drago.

"Can you contact your friend Paul Guillaume?"

"I will try to reach him. What's up?"

"Something has to be done about getting the ambassador's daughter back. I have a plan, and your friend could help us pull it off."

"Before I make this call. Will you compensate Paul for helping us?" David asked. "Money goes a long way with getting things done here."

"Money is no object."

"Good," David said and put the call through to Paul. "If I reach him, where should we meet?"

"I'm open to any suggestions you have about a meeting place once it is secure."

"I know such a place."

"Good. Then make the arrangements!" Drago and David meet with Paul at the prearranged place.

"What's the plan? David mentioned that you have a plan," Paul inquired.

"We know they will transport Rudy Auckerman from his cell in Croix des Bouquets to the Court House in Rue Mgr Guilloux early tomorrow morning with one patrol car as an escort," Drago said.

"So," Paul said with skepticism in his voice.

"We will hit them in Tabarre and take the

prisoner," Drago explained, pointing out the location on the map to David and Paul.

"You know. That will work. Not much is happening that time of the day in Tabarre," Paul said.

Huge, dark clouds covered the early morning sky. It was humid even before the sun rose.

It was going to rain sometime today. The rain was up there behind those dark clouds.

They executed the plan with precision. Using an unmarked embassy vehicle, David got between the escort car and the utility van carrying the prisoner Rudy Auckerman.

Drago, David, and Paul wore face masks, with only the eyes exposed.

Drago was riding a shotgun with David. Paul followed the vehicle transporting the prisoner.

David pushed the escort car off the road, rendering it disabled. He slowed down to ensure there wasn't enough room for the van to pass. Both vehicles came to a stop.

"Mr. Gibson, how many guards would you estimate are in that van?"

"Two, maybe three at the most."

"And there's three of us I'd say that's about even. Won't you say?"

The fixer looked at him. David was more hyper than fearful, under the influence of the surging adrenaline. His hands gripped the steering wheel tight, causing the knuckles to turn white.

"What exactly do you do? If I may inquire?" David asked.

"You arrived at the embassy, and the staff is at your disposal."

Without an answer, Drago got out and walked to the van carrying the prisoner holding the LCR.38 with the sound compressor attached in both hands with the driver in his sights.

Paul came up on the passenger side and motioned for them to open the door to the prisoner.

After a discussion between the driver and his partner, the door opened. Paul entered with a bolt cutter and freed Rudy Auckerman from the chains on his hands and ankles.

They handcuffed Rudy and put him in the back of the unmarked embassy vehicle, and sped away from the scene.

Drago had shot out both front tires of the vehicles transporting the prisoner.

No one was injured during the breakout of the prisoner Rudy Auckerman. The exchange was to be at 08.00 in one of the abandoned warehouses in 'Cite Soleil'.

"What now?" David asked as they sped away.

"Go to the exchange rendezvous. We should reach there first to scout the area for any snipers they may have in position," Drago instructed.

"I was thinking the same thing."

"Let Paul know we are heading to the warehouse!"

David contacted Paul on the cell phone and told him where they were heading.

"The ambassador's daughter. Does she know who you are?" Drago asked.

"Yes. She does. Although she's been here for a short time."

"I never got her name."

"Her name is Jo-Anne McArthur."

"What about her mother?"

"The ambassador is a widower, lost his wife a few years ago to cancer."

"I see."

"After losing her mother, Jo-Anne got into drugs and spiraled out of control," David said.

"At the exchange. I want you and Paul to handle it. I would find a vantage point to cover you to avoid surprises from her captives."

Reaching the warehouse, Drago got out of vehicle, leaving David alone with the prisoner Rudy Auckerman, with Paul close behind.

Paul parked his car on a side street close to the warehouse and walked the rest of the way to the meeting place.

After the exchange, Paul was to leave before the vehicle carrying the prisoner Rudy Auckerman. His job was to tail them and relay information back to Drago.

If all goes as planned, the fixer and his team will retake the prisoner Rudy Auckerman and hand him back to the police.

The time was seven fifteen, Forty-five minutes before the arranged time for the exchange.

Drago was scouring the high ledges of the building when a flash from a glass caught his eyes. The fixer made his way to the position where the flash came from.

As the fixer got closer, it didn't surprise him to see a gunner lying on his stomach, looking through the scope of a long-range rifle with a sound suppressor attached.

The gunner was adjusting the scope. He didn't hear or see the fixer until he felt the cold muzzle of a weapon at the back of his head. Then everything went back as the bullet entered his skull.

Drago pulled the dead man away from the gutter by the collar of his shirt. Then he took the dead man's rifle by the nozzle and hit it against the edge of a bolder, smashing it into pieces.

The fixer walked around the ruins of the warehouse. Satisfied that no other gunners were hiding, he returned to the area where the sniper was and took his position.

Jo-Anne's kidnappers arrived in two vehicles. The first one carried the man in charge, he was a medium-height, black man, dressed in white pants and a shirt with a red pandora on his head, in the company of two gunners, and the next van had Jo-Anne with a driver and one other gunner.

The swap went off without incident.

They drug the Ambassador's daughter. She did not know where she was, or who was rescuing her.

Drago joined David after the kidnappers left the area.

"This is Mr. Gibson, the man responsible for your safe return," David explained to Jo-Anne.

The girl was slowly coming around. What they gave her was wearing off.

Jo-Anne extended her right hand. "Thank you, Mr. Gibson, sir," she said as Drago took her trembling hand.

After the exchange, David called the ambassador and informed him to meet him at the prearranged place to take his daughter.

Paul followed the van carrying Rudy Auckerman to a building in Delmas.

Drago and David caught up with Paul after dropping off Jo-Anne.

The building was three stories high and had six feet high walls with cameras mounted on the corners.

The fixer went prone and surveyed the building. Cameras mounted only in the front corners of the building. Drago moved along the south wall and spotted an open window on the second floor.

Under the widow was a metal trellis covered in climbing hydrangea. The fixer seized the opportunity and climbed onto the trellis.

Reaching the widow, he looked inside. The prisoner, Rudy Auckerman, was sitting at a table in front of a computer with two gunners standing behind him.

At another table to the right of Auckerman, four other black men sat playing a game of dominos with rifles up against an unoccupied chair.

Not wanting to be seen, the fixer quietly climbed down the trellis and rejoined David and Paul.

"How does it look?" David asked.

"The prisoner is in the building."

"And gunners? how many are in there with him?"Paul inquired.

"I counted six, but there could be more," Drago replied.

"What about the man giving the orders at the

exchange? Was he there?"

"If he is there, he could be in another part of the building."

"Paul believes this is the work of the newly arrived Jamaicans," David said.

Drago's cell phone buzzed. He answered and listened to the voice on the other end without interrupting. After a few moments and many uh huhs, Drago turned off the cell.

"The prisoner Rudy Auckerman is an Irish/American. His mother was Irish, and his father was American," Drago informed David and Paul.

"So what?" Paul asked.

"When Auckerman's plane went down, it was carrying something important for the Irish that's the reason they wanted to get Rudy out of prison. He is the only one who knows the passcode to get the information from the computer," Drago explained.

"What's your plan to get Rudy back in jail?" Paul asked.

"Do you think that we'll need help?" David asked.

"We will let the police deal with the capture of the fugitive. Paul can tip off his friends at the station. We will keep Rudy and his buddies from leaving," Drago said.

Things sometimes don't go as planned.

David was looking through a pair of binoculars.

"There's a silver Cadillac SUV just pulled up at the front of the building," David said.

Drago took the binoculars from David and watched as four men got out of the vehicle.

"He is here," Drago said, seeing the person was in charge of the exchange.

"Maybe Rudy successfully retrieved the information from the computer," David suggested.

"We have to go after them now," Paul suggested.

"It's ten of them and only three of us," David said.

From the care package in the boot of the unmarked embassy vehicle, David took out three grenades, giving one each to Drago and Paul.

The three men left the vehicle. Paul took the front, David went to the door at the south side of the building, and the fixer climbed the trellis up to the window on the second floor.

Paul and David blew open the doors at the front and side of the building in sequence. Drago threw his grenade through the window,it activated a few seconds after the doors blew open.

Paul and David went through the doors in crouched positions, holding their rifle with both hands. David moved along the south wall. Paul moved to his left, taking out gunners, so as not to be caught in each other crossfire.

Drago entered through the window. He sprayed a few bullets, hitting the floor to distract the group of men guarding the prisoner. The two gunners turned their attention to the upper open window where Drago had fired his weapon from.

## Chapter Sixteen

The first shot shattered the glass over the fixer's head. Pieces of the shattered window fell on Drago as he pivoted to the right. Suddenly, rounds of bullets were drilling against the wall and punching holes. The fixer ducked, bullets whizzing over his head.

"Get him!" the man in charge shouted.

The fixer shifted again and moved to the staircase leading to the lower floor. He fired three rounds, hitting two of the gunners as the men fell to their knees. Drago discarded the rifle and drew the LCR.38.

The three men with Uzis pinned Paul and David down. Drago followed a trail of blood leading away from the table where the prisoner Rudy Auckerman sat earlier working on the computer.

The blood trail led Drago to the prisoner and another man hiding behind the door of another office. Both men were bleeding from gunshot wounds. The fixer secured the two men's hands and feet with plastic zip ties.

Drago searched through both men's pockets. Papers in the man's pockets identify him as Levi Butcher, a Jamaican national. the mini disk and pocketed it.

Leaving them in the office, Drago followed the sound of the gunfire. The fixer saw Paul, signaling to where David was. Paul fired at the men with the Uzi's having them give their positions away and gave cover to Drago as he moved in a crouched position to get behind the gunners.

Drago fired at the two men to his right, hitting one of them in the neck and the other in the chest. The gunner dropped the Uzi and held his neck with both hands as the blood squirted between his fingers.

Paul and David took out the third gunner when he tried to move away from his position after Drago shot the two members of his team.

"What about the prisoner?" Paul asked after he and David joined Drago.

"They are in an office back there."

"You said they. Who is with Rudy?" David inquired.

"The man in charge. Levi Butcher along with Rudy," Drago explained.

"The cops will be here shortly. I just called them," Paul said.

"Paul. You and I must go," Drago said after retrieving the rifle he had discarded earlier.

"You should receive a promotion for recapturing the prisoner," David said, tapping Paul on his shoulder.

"Get out of here. I will talk to you later," Paul stated.

The fixer and David left Paul with the two men and headed to the embassy.

"Levi Butcher. Do you have anything on him?" the fixer asked David when they pulled away from the building.

"No. I don't think so. I'll run a check when we get to the embassy."

The fixer put the tools of his trade back into the care package in the boot of the embassy vehicle, patted the pocket of his trousers to be sure the USB drive was still there, and then sat in the passenger seat next to David.

"Levi Butcher. Do you have anything on him?" the fixer asked David when they pulled away from the building.

"No. I don't think so. I'll run a check when we get to the embassy." Sirens were wailing somewhere in the distance. Paul got busy checking for a pulse on the slain gunners. He found a couple of men with pulses and decided not to move the wounded men for fear that moving them may do more damage to the injury they sustained.

At the embassy, the doctor worked on Jo-Anne. The young woman had scars on her back and thighs. He was still monitoring her condition when David and Drago arrived.

Ambassador McArthur greeted the Agents and took them into his office. "My daughter has asked about the people who rescued her."

"How is she?" David asked.

"The doctor is with her. She is resting."

"She is young. I hope she pulls through," Drago said.

"Will you be heading back to New York? Or stay here for a few days?" McArthur asked.

"Not staying. I will head back to NY, then to London."

"I can't thank both of you enough for bringing my daughter back to me alive."

"It all comes with the job," the fixer replied. "I must have an official report on what took place at the exchange."

"David can prepare that for you," Drago stated.

The fixer takes the USB drive with him to New York and has it deciphered by the tech.

Today was a great day for the good guys. No lives were lost. Who knows what tomorrow will be?

The battle for control of the drug trade on

the islands will continue. Who will win? As of today, no one knows.

These paradise islands in the Caribbean were slowly becoming a battleground for control of the drug trade. Drago, and the other members of the A.W.B. aka "Agents Without Borders" will do whatever it takes to combat the situation.

Other books by Sherwin A Goodman

Rick Drago "In The Tropics"
Rick Drago "The Missing Prototype"
David Trent
Structures Of In-elegance
A Summer At Sea
Caribbean Assassin
Susan & Friends Crosstown
Barbados Heroine
Samuel Higgins "The Asian Affair"